PRAISE FOR

SCU

"I've had the pleasure of watching SCURRY grow from its humble beginnings to the incredible saga it is today. It is hands-down panel for panel one of the most beautiful books you will ever experience. It's hard to separate the book from the creator, Mac Smith, who is the creative tour de force who single handedly brought this world to life. When you discover a series of books like SCURRY it's kind of magical...savor this book, it is a rare and wonderful creation from the heart of a very unique creative voice!"

JOHN MUELLER
Art Director, Blizzard Entertainment, *Diablo III, IV*

"Thrilling and heartwarming. Bold storytelling with rich, emotive artwork that'll take you back to your favorite VHS clamshell. *The Secret of Nimh* meets *The Road*. Highly recommended! Scurry out and find yourself a copy!"

TONY FLEECS
Writer/co-creator of *Stray Dogs*

"I loved it--a gorgeously painted world rich with life, where complex animal societies and mythologies bring to mind the classic *Watership Down*. Never have I wanted a moose friend so badly."

IRMA KNIIVILA
EVERYDAY HERO MACHINE BOY

"What an epic and lavishly painted adventure! I loved everything about it: the good animals, the bad animals, the mythology, the hauntingly familiar setting. ALL OF IT!"

TRI VUONG
EVERYDAY HERO MACHINE BOY, LEGO® NINJAGO®: GARMADON

"Smith has given us a ferocious tale of adventure, danger, and friendship presented in glorious artwork. Never have such small heroes loomed so large on the page!"

MATTHEW CODY
Award-winning Author of *Powerless* and *Cat Ninja*

"Deeply cinematic and packed to the brim with an unrivaled sense of scale and true danger. Smith has created a rich and engrossing world with the gravitas and weight of classical mythology, all taking place in your backyard."

To Mom, Dad,
and my brothers.

SCURRY

MAC SMITH

The World of SCURRY
Hawk's Nest
The Mountain
The Dead Forest
The Refuge
The Lodge
Drowned Town
Beaver Dam
Wolf Migrations
Guardian's Cave
Pict's Journey
Gorgon's Lair
Cursed Coast
Wix's Journey
Wild Mice
The Overpass
The CITY
Skoga's Den
The Suburbs
Atlas Meets Wix
The Colony
Shady Run Lane
The Neighborhood
N
E
W
S

"But, Mousie, thou art not alone,
In proving foresight may be vain;
The best-laid schemes o' mice an 'men
Oft go awry..."

-ROBERT BURNS
To a Mouse

PART I

LINGERING LIGHT

"WE CAME ALL THE WAY OUT HERE FOR *THIS* HEAP?"
"I GOT A GOOD FEELING ABOUT THIS ONE!"
"YOU SAID THAT ABOUT THE LAST THREE HOUSES."
THIS WAY!
SNIF
SNIF

ALL CLEAR.
WHAT A DUMP.
YOU THINK THERE'S ANY FOOD IN HERE, WIX?
DOUBT IT, BUT WE HAVE TO CHECK ANYWAY. GOTTA FIND SOMETHING FOR THE COLONY.

WASN'T SEEP AND HIS CREW SUPPOSED TO HIT THIS PLACE LAST WEEK?

SEEP? DUNNO. NO ONE'S HEARD FROM HIM IN AWHILE.

WHAT'S THAT...

SMELL?

JACKPOT!

TOLD YA I HAD A GOOD FEELI--

UMF, NO!!!
DROP IT, YOU DOPE!
HUH?

IT'S POISON!!

DANGER!

P-POISON? ARE YOU SURE?
I THINK IT LOOKS FINE.
OH, *YOU* THINK IT'S FINE? OK THEN. DON'T LISTEN TO *ME*...
JUST LIKE *EKT* DIDN'T LISTEN TO ME.
EKT...
...
-sigh-
WELL, I'M NOT *THAT* HUNGRY ANYWAY.
HOW DO YOU ALWAYS *KNOW*, WIX?
JUST COME ON, UMF. THROUGH HERE.

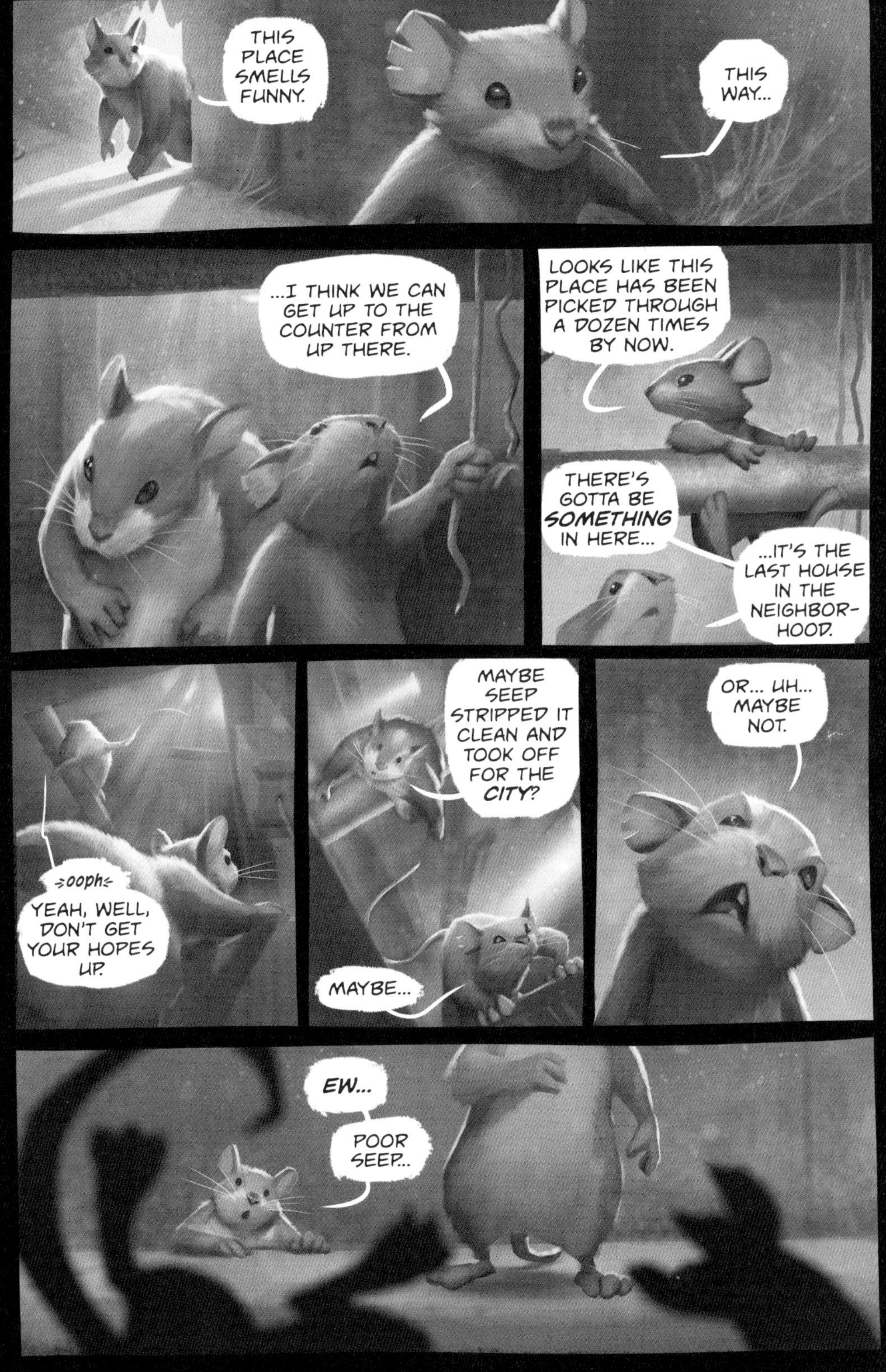
THIS PLACE SMELLS FUNNY.
THIS WAY...
...I THINK WE CAN GET UP TO THE COUNTER FROM UP THERE.
LOOKS LIKE THIS PLACE HAS BEEN PICKED THROUGH A DOZEN TIMES BY NOW.
THERE'S GOTTA BE SOMETHING IN HERE...
...IT'S THE LAST HOUSE IN THE NEIGHBOR-HOOD.
ooph
YEAH, WELL, DON'T GET YOUR HOPES UP.
MAYBE SEEP STRIPPED IT CLEAN AND TOOK OFF FOR THE CITY?
MAYBE...
OR... UH... MAYBE NOT.
EW...
POOR SEEP...

SEEP NEVER COULD LEAVE THESE TRAPS ALONE.
I WARNED HIM A THOUSAND TIMES...
YUCK!
HOW DID HE GET TWISTED AROUND LIKE THAT?
DUNNO. HE MUST HAVE TRIED, TO ROLL OUT OF THE WAY.
THE BAIT'S STILL UNDER HIM. NO SENSE LETTING IT GO TO WASTE.
SORRY, SEEP. YA SHOULDA LET THIS ONE GO.

UH... WHAT IS IT?
IT WAS CHEESE... I THINK. IT MIGHT STILL BE EDIBLE.
LET'S KEEP MOVING.
WOW! LOOK AT THAT!
DOESN'T THAT LOOK DELICIOUS!
IT'S PLASTIC YOU KNOW.
YEAH, I KNOW, WIX, I'M NOT THAT DUMB.
WHY DO YOU THINK THEY KEPT FAKE FOOD AROUND?
MAYBE TO TRICK US...
TO LURE US OUT IN THE OPEN SO THEY CAN SPLAT US!
OR DISTRACT US WHILE THEY HIDE THE REAL STUFF? WHO KNOWS?
ANYWAY, WE HAVE A LOT OF CABINETS TO SEARCH...
"WE BETTER HURRY...
"...THE CATS WILL BE OUT SOON."

THE COLONY...
KEEP OUT
PICT, COME INSIDE.
IT'S COLD...
...AND THERE IS TALK OF A HAWK ABOUT.
OH, HELLO, DAD. DON'T WORRY. NO BIRDS OUT TODAY.
I CAN SEE EVERYTHING FROM UP HERE.
NOT AS WELL AS THAT HAWK...
...IT CAN SWOOP RIGHT OUT OF THE CLOUDS AND SNATCH UP A MOUSE BEFORE SHE KNOWS WHAT HIT HER.
IT'S NOT THAT CLOUDY. LOOK! THE SUN IS OUT! I CAN'T REMEMBER THE LAST TIME I SAW IT. MAYBE IT WILL GET WARMER SOON!
HMM... MAYBE IT WILL... BUT WE'VE BEEN FOOLED BEFORE.
HAS EVERYONE RETURNED FROM THEIR SCAVENGING?

EVERYONE IS BACK BUT WIX AND HIS BIG RAT FRIEND, BUT THEY'RE **ALWAYS** LATE.
INDEED, THOUGH THEY HAD THE FARTHEST TO GO. MAYBE WE SHOULDN'T HAVE SENT THEM OUT SO FAR.
WHAT CHOICE WAS THERE? THERE'S NOTHING LEFT AROUND HERE. BESIDES, HE'S OUR BEST SCAVENGER, OR SO **HE** ALWAYS TELLS ME.
HEHEH, IT SHOULDN'T BE ANY TROUBLE FOR OUR *"BEST"* THEN.
DAD, WHAT IS IT?
MAYBE THE ELDERS AND I MADE A MISTAKE KEEPING THE COLONY HERE SO LONG.
I THOUGHT IT WOULD BE WARMER BY NOW... BUT THIS WINTER... IT HAS LINGERED TOO LONG. IT'S SO STRANGE, PICT... I'VE NEVER SEEN ANYTHING LIKE IT.
I THOUGHT WE COULD WAIT FOR SPRING TO MOVE ON, OR PERHAPS THE **HUMANS** WOULD FINALLY RETURN...
BUT SPRING DOESN'T COME, AND WHO KNOWS WHERE THE HUMANS WENT.
WE CAN'T HOLD OUT HERE MUCH LONGER. MORE GET SICK EVERY DAY, AND OUR FOOD IS RUNNING OUT.

WE'D STILL HAVE PLENTY IF RESHER'S ***LACKEYS*** WEREN'T SKIMMING FROM THE STORE ROOMS... AND THE GUARDS WEREN'T SITTING AROUND DOING ***NOTHING***!

THEY ARE JUST AFRAID, PICT. THE COLONY IS GETTING DESPERATE, BUT WE ***MUST*** NOT TURN ON EACH OTHER.

YES, FATHER, BUT--

ahem

EH?

MASTER ORIM, PICT, I'M SORRY TO INTERRUPT, BUT THE OTHERS ARE READY TO START.

OH, OF COURSE, KESSEL, I'LL BE RIGHT THERE.

I'M COMING, TOO. I HAVE A FEW THINGS TO SAY TO ***RESHER*** AND HIS CRONIES.

ELSEWHERE...
FIND ANYTHING, UMF?
NOPE. YOU?
NOPE.
-sigh- THIS PLACE IS DEAD.
BREAK OUT THAT CHEESE. WE CAN SPLIT IT.
YOU KNOW THE RULES, UMF. EVERY-THING GOES BACK TO THE COLONY.
OH, COME ON, WIX! THAT LITTLE CRUMB ISN'T GOING TO--
SHH! DO YOU HEAR SOMETHI--?
GET DOWN!
ching
ching

snip snip
ching ching
WHO IS IT?
IT'S JUST DUMB OLE ORK. WE CAN SNEAK RIGHT BY HER.
OH GREAT. SCRATCHER'S STILL FOLLOWING HER AROUND...
NO DOUBT CHASING DOWN WHATEVER ORK'S BELL SCARES OUT.
I HEARD THEY GOT MOOCH LAST WEEK.
MOOCH WAS OLD AND BLIND. IT WAS ONLY A MATTER OF TIME BEFORE SOMETHING GOT HIM.
WE CAN HANDLE THESE TWO.
ching ching
HSSSSSSSSSS

SHOULD WE GO BACK THE WAY WE CAME?
UGH! WE'LL BE HERE ALL NIGHT WAITING ON THEM TO LEAVE...
hmm...
LOOK! IF WE CAN GET TO THE WINDOW, WE'LL BE HOME FREE!
I DON'T KNOW, WIX...
IT'LL BE NO PROBLEM, UMF! WE'LL SLIP ACROSS THE COUNTER, HOP ON THE FRIDGE DOOR, THEN RIGHT OUT THE WINDOW!
OKAY, LET'S JUST GET OUT OF HERE.
FOLLOW ME!
HURRY!

I THINK ONE OF THEM IS ON OUR SCENT--
WAK!
oof
UH-OH.
CRASH!
oops.
!?
LOOK OUT!

ACK!!

CRASH

BACK TO THE HOLE!

ALMOST THERE!
HURRY!

REEAWWWRR!

BETTER
LUCK NEXT TIME,
LOSERS!
WOOOOOSH
SWING
ALMOST TO
THE WINDOW!
WHAT THE--?

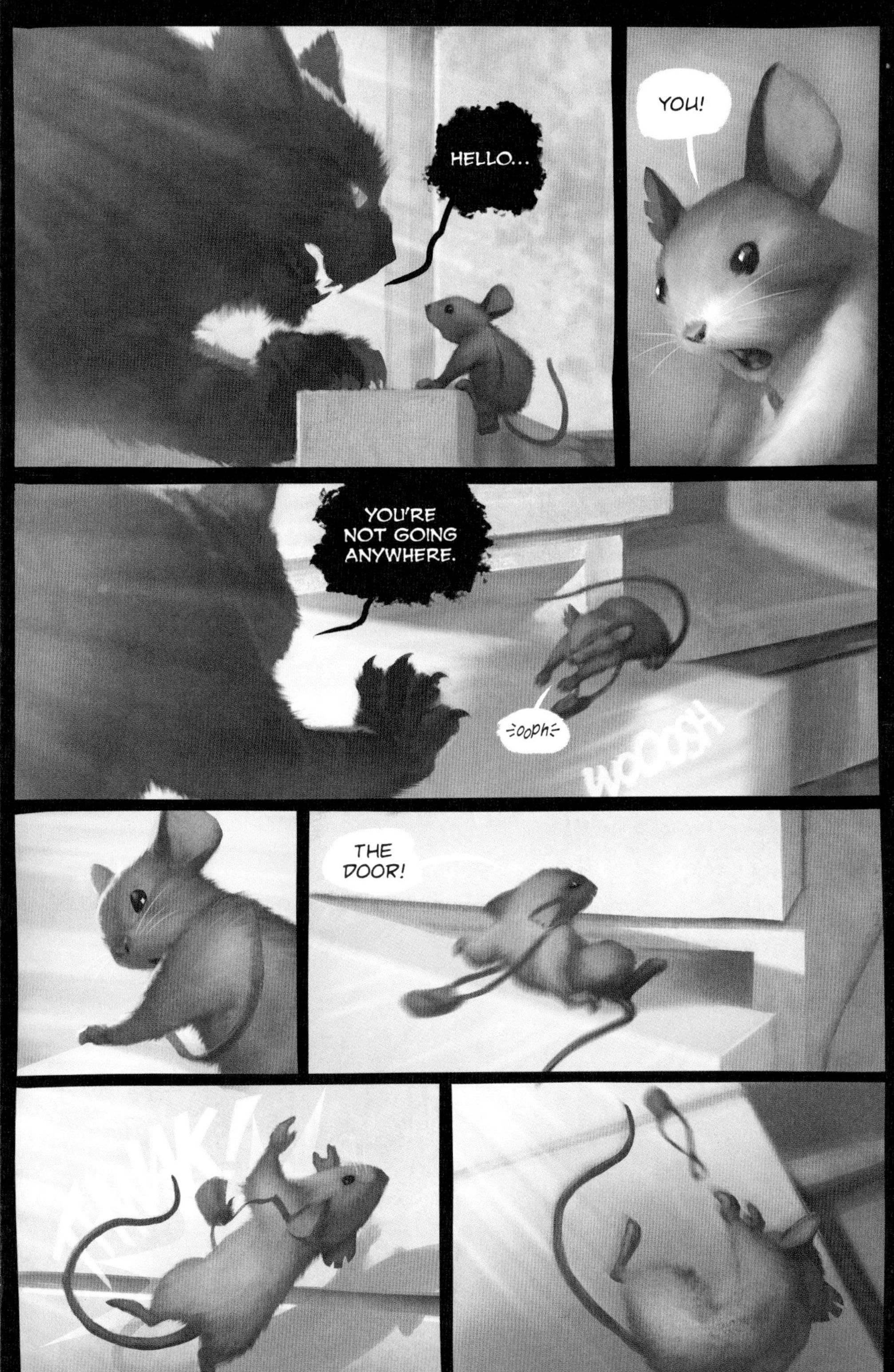
HELLO...
YOU!
YOU'RE NOT GOING ANYWHERE.
ooph
WOOOSH
THE DOOR!

BAM
BAM
Oooooooooh--*

WIX!

COME ON, GET UP...
GET UP!
COULD IT BE?

YES! IT IS YOU!
THE ONE WHO GOT AWAY...

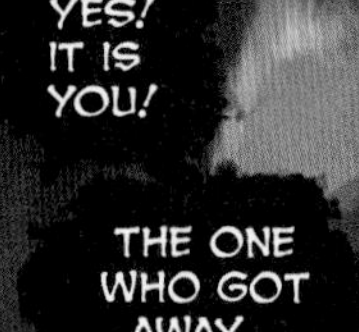

WELL... NOT ALL OF YOU.

TITAN!

BACK AT THE COLONY...
THERE IS NO MORE TIME! WE MUST RELOCATE TO THE CITY AT ONCE!
FOR ALL WE KNOW IT'S AS BAD THERE AS HERE! MAYBE WORSE!
NONE OF THE SCOUTS WE'VE SENT TO THE CITY HAVE RETURNED, RESHER.
RETURN HERE!? TO ALL THIS? WHY WOULD THEY RETURN WHEN THEY HAVE EVERYTHING THEY NEED OVER THERE?
THEY WOULDN'T JUST LEAVE AND NOT COME BACK!
WE DON'T EVEN KNOW IF THEY REACHED THE CITY.
THEN WHAT CHANCE WOULD WE HAVE? WE HAVE SICK AND INJURED!
IF WE LEAVE NOW, TOGETHER, WITH WHAT WE HAVE LEFT, WE HAVE A MUCH GREATER CHANCE OF REACHING THE CITY THAN A FEW SCOUTS!
YES, THE JOURNEY WILL BE DIFFICULT, BUT MOST OF US WILL MAKE IT.
MOST OF US!? WHAT ABOUT THE ONES THAT DON'T?

SHOULD WE ALL STAY HERE AND STARVE BECAUSE WE COULDN'T MAKE THE TOUGH DECISIONS?
WE CAN'T MARCH THE ENTIRE COLONY OFF TO THE CITY BASED ON YOUR BLIND HOPE THAT THE HUMANS WILL BE THERE TO PROVIDE FOR US.
BUT IF WE STAY AND THE HUMANS DON'T RETURN, WHAT THEN?
OH, HERE IT COMES...
WE DON'T HAVE TO DEPEND ON THEM AT ALL!
WE HAVE ALWAYS LIVED ALONGSIDE THE HUMANS, PICT. IT IS OUR WAY AND IT HAS ALWAYS SERVED US.
AND NOW THEY ARE GONE!
BUT WE CAN LOOK ELSEWHERE! THERE MAY BE FOOD IN THE NEARBY FIELDS, AND IN THE FOREST--
AGAIN WITH THE FOREST!? YOU WANT US TO LIVE LIKE THE BARBARIANS, WALLOWING IN THE MUD AND SCRAPING FOR SEEDS? LIVING IN CONSTANT FEAR OF BEING DEVOURED BY SOME WILD BEAST? WE ARE ABOVE SUCH A LIFE.
HOW IS THIS ANY BETTER!? SURVIVING ON POISON SCRAPS FROM BEINGS THAT CEASELESSLY TRY TO KILL US!?
ALRIGHT, I THINK WE'VE HEARD ENOUGH FOR TODAY. WE WILL CONTINUE THIS DISCUSSION IN THE MORNING.
THAT IS ALL.
WONDERFUL, MORE TALK.

MEANWHILE...

HE HAS HIM NOW!

HHMPH!

I GOTTA DO SOMETHING!

!

NO RUNNING TODAY, MOUSE?

THAT'S NO FUN.

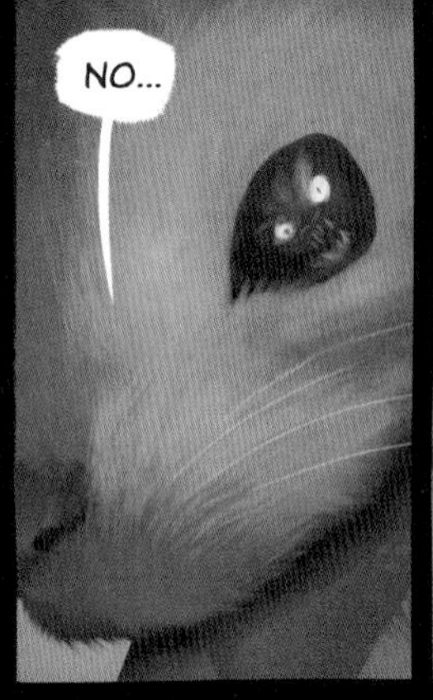

GOODBYE, MOUSE.

COME ON... =hrghh= ...LITTLE... ...MORE...
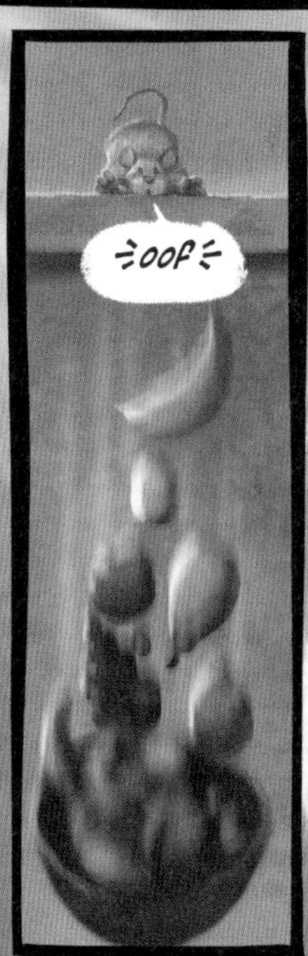
=oof=

BONG
KAKH
BAM
BOING
BOING
BANG
RRRREEOW!

WE'RE UNDER ATTACK-- OOPH!

GET OFF ME, YOU IDIOT!
BING
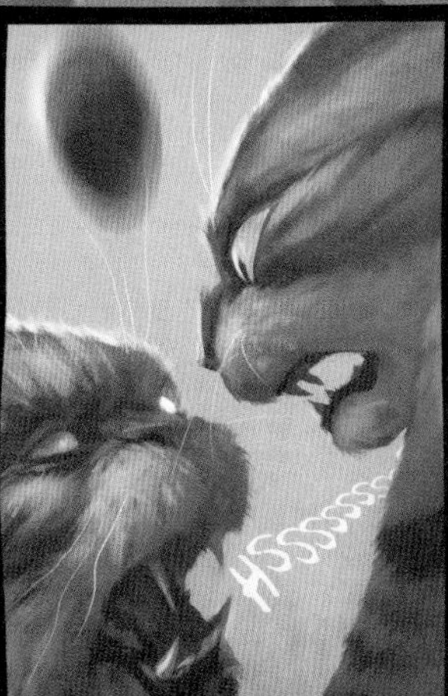
HSSSSSS

BOING
EH?
COME BACK!
IT'S A TRICK!
GO, GO, GO!
HUH?
NO!
NOT AGAIN!!!

OUTSIDE...
WHAT ARE THOSE IDIOTS DOING IN THERE?
PROBABLY FIGHTING AGAIN. LET'S GO WATCH.

IS THAT A--?

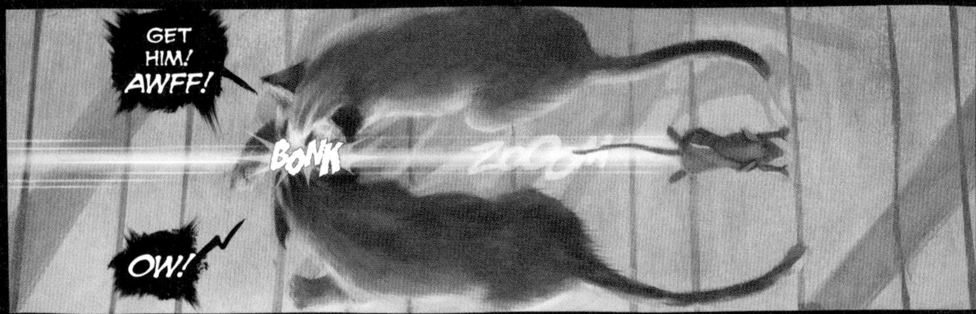
GET HIM! AWFF!
BONK
OW!

CRASH

MOVE!

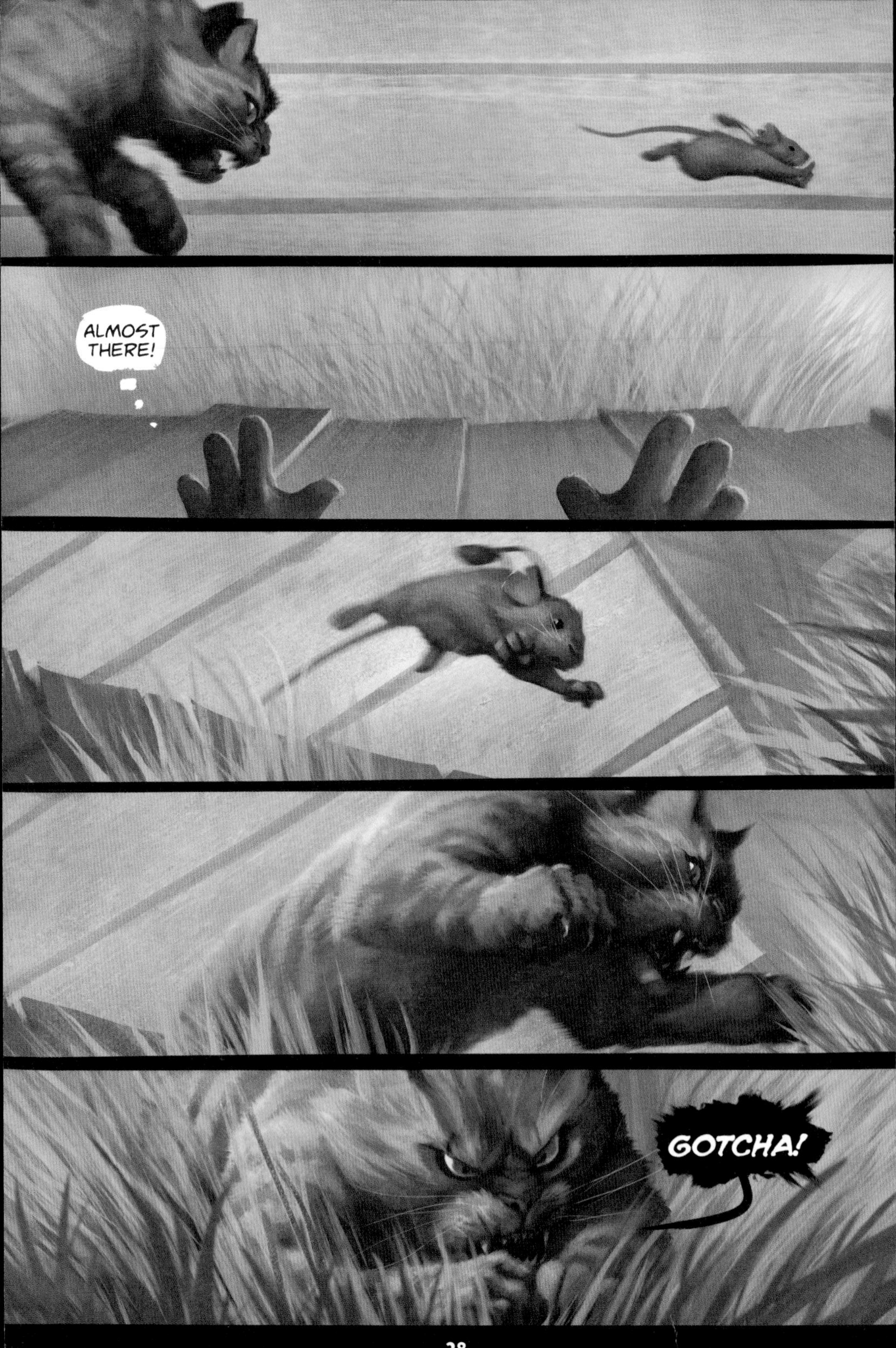
ALMOST THERE!
GOTCHA!

EH?!
NNNOOOOOOOOOO
-phew-
CLOSE ONE!
THE FENCE!
THERE'S MY EXIT!
SNIFF
SNIFF
SNIFF
BETTER LUCK NEXT TIME, YOU STUPID CAT!

WHA--?

IT'S **GONE!**

HEY! THERE YOU ARE! YOU MADE IT!
GAH!
WHY ARE YOU JUST LAYING THERE?
DON'T SNEAK UP ON ME LIKE THAT!
OK, OK. SHEESH. LET'S JUST GET OUT OF HERE.
NO! NOT THAT WAY!
FOLLOW ME. WE'LL GO AROUND.
HUH? WHY THIS WAY?
JUST COME ON!

"TRUST ME...
"...YOU DON'T WANT TO GO THAT WAY."

PART II

BEASTS OF WINTER

THE NEXT MORNING, JUST OUTSIDE THE COLONY HOUSE...
I CAN'T WAIT TO BE INSIDE. I'M STARVING
...
OH, COME ON, WIX, YOU CAN'T *STILL* BE MAD AT ME!
YOU ALMOST GOT ME *KILLED!*
YEAH, BUT THEN I SAVED YOU!
I HAD IT UNDER CONTROL.
YEAH RIGHT. YOU WERE A GONER UNTIL I DROPPED THAT BOWL ON THEIR HEADS.
DID YOU SEE THEIR FACES? WHO KNEW CATS WERE SO AFRAID OF FRUIT?
-HAH!- YEAH, I ADMIT THAT WAS PRETTY FUNNY. OLD TITAN NEARLY HAD A HEART ATTACK!
LET'S JUST HURRY BACK. THEY PROBABLY THINK WE'RE DEAD BY NOW.

INSIDE, ANOTHER MEETING TAKES PLACE...
THE ELDERS ARE IN AGREEMENT.
THERE IS ENOUGH FOOD FOR NOW IF WE RATION, AND SPRING WILL ARRIVE SOON.
WE MUST NOT ACT RASHLY BY BLINDLY SENDING OUR FAMILIES INTO DANGER.
THEREFORE, WE WILL CONTINUE TO EXPLORE THE SURROUNDING AREAS, AND WAIT FOR THE RETURN OF OUR SCOUTS SENT TO THE CITY.
IF WE ARE PATIENT, A SOLUTION WILL PRESENT ITSELF, AND THEN WE CAN ACT WITH MORE CERTAINTY.
NO...
NO MORE WAITING...
I WILL NOT SIT HERE DOING NOTHING WHILE WE STARVE! MY MICE WILL GO TO THE CITY, AND ANYONE WHO WANTS TO THRIVE CAN COME WITH US!
RESHER!
YOU CAN'T DO THIS! YOU CANNOT DIVIDE THE COLONY! OUR NEST WILL NEVER FOLLOW YOU!
YOU WILL ONLY SLOW US DOWN, RAT! OUR NEST WILL GO WITH RESHER, A REAL LEADER!
YOU WON'T TAKE OUR FOOD WITH YOU!
WE WILL TAKE WHAT IS OURS!
ahem
IF I MAY INTERRUPT...

...I BELIEVE I CAN OFFER AN ALTERNATIVE COURSE OF ACTION.
OF COURSE, KESSEL, GO AHEAD.
THANK YOU.
I'M SURE YOU'VE ALL HEARD THE RUMORS OF THE WRECKED VEHICLE THE HUMANS USED TO TRANSPORT FOOD.
HMM?
THE TRUCK? I'VE HEARD THERE WAS ONE NEAR THE HIGHWAY... IS IT REALLY THERE?
YES. IT IS.
WHY ARE WE ONLY HEARING ABOUT THIS NOW?
I JUST CONFIRMED IT THIS MORNING...
"ONE OF MY SCOUTS RETURNED FROM THE AREA LAST NIGHT.
"HE CLAIMED THAT THE DOORS WERE SHUT, BUT A TREE HAD FALLEN AND GOUGED A SMALL HOLE IN THE SIDE...
"INSIDE, HE SAW DOZENS OF BOXES STREWN ABOUT."

WHERE IS THIS SCOUT? LET US HEAR WHAT HE HAS TO SAY.
HE WAS BADLY MAULED BY A CAT DURING HIS RETURN. HE BARELY MADE IT BACK AT ALL.
I'M AFRAID HE DIED SHORTLY AFTER RETURNING, BUT BEFORE HE DID HE SWORE THAT THE TRUCK WAS THERE.
HE WAS INJURED. MAYBE HE WAS DELIRIOUS?
BUT IF IT'S TRUE, WE COULD LIVE ON THE CONTENTS FOR MONTHS! IT'S WORTH CHECKING OUT.
IF IT'S REALLY THERE, THAT'S QUITE A LONG WAY AND YOU'LL HAVE TO CUT THROUGH PART OF THE WOODS TO GET TO IT.
THE WOODS...
IT WILL BE A DIFFICULT TRIP, BUT ONCE WE CLEAR THE FOREST, WE SHOULD BE FREE OF THE WORST DANGER.
I BELIEVE WE CAN BE THERE IN TWO DAYS.
IF WE FIND SOMETHING, I'LL SEND A RUNNER BACK WHILE WE GATHER THE CARGO.
RESHER, WILL YOU AGREE TO WAIT WHILE WE INVESTIGATE THIS "TRUCK"?
FINE, BUT WE WILL NOT ACCEPT ANY MORE DELAYS. YOU HAVE **FOUR** DAYS--TWO THERE AND TWO BACK--AND **NO** MORE.
GOOD. THEN IT'S SETTLED. KESSEL, GATHER YOUR SCOUTS. YOU LEAVE THIS AFTERNOON.
YOU WILL NEED TO CLEAR THE LAWNS BEFORE THE CATS ARE STIRRING.
I'LL ASSEMBLE OUR BEST.

IF THERE IS NOTHING ELSE, THIS MEETING IS ADJOURNED.

THANK YOU, KESSEL. YOU MAY HAVE BOUGHT US SOME TIME.
LET'S JUST HOPE THERE IS SOMETHING FOR US TO BRING BACK.

DAD, KESSEL, I WOULD LIKE TO GO WITH THE PARTY TO THE HIGHWAY.
ABSOLUTELY NOT.

IF WE ARE GOING THROUGH THE FOREST, WE COULD POSSIBLY MAKE CONTACT WITH THE TRIBES THERE! WE--
THE WILD ONES IN THE FOREST WON'T HELP US, PICT. THEY ARE NOT CIVILISED.

OH, I DON'T KNOW... MAYBE IT WOULD BE A GOOD IDEA FOR HER TO EXPERIENCE THE FOREST FIRSTHAND?
STAY OUT OF THIS, RESHER!

FATHER, I--
ENOUGH! ALL OF YOU! cough cough I HAVE MADE MY DECISION. KESSEL, GET YOUR MICE READY. cough

ARE YOU ALRIGHT?
YES cough YES, I AM FINE, PICT. I'M JUST A BIT TIRED.

I CAN'T STAY LOCKED UP IN HERE FOREVER! I DON'T NEED YOU TO PROTECT ME.
I'M NOT PROTECTING YOU. I NEED YOU HERE.
WHAT? WHY?
=cough= WITH KESSEL AND OUR MOST LOYAL SCOUTS GONE, I NEED SOMEONE HERE I CAN TRUST.
RESHER IS UP TO SOMETHING, BUT I DON'T KNOW WHAT.
HE WANTED ME TO GO...
YES.
WHAT WILL THE ELDERS DO IF RESHER AND HIS FOLLOWERS DECIDE TO LEAVE?
LET THEM GO, I SUPPOSE. WE CAN'T MAKE THEM STAY. BUT I THINK RESHER MAY HAVE OTHER THINGS IN MIND.
HE MAY BE RIGHT, YOU KNOW. WE CAN'T STAY HERE MUCH LONGER.
PERHAPS, BUT TOO MANY ARE SICK TO MAKE SUCH A LONG TRIP RIGHT NOW.
AND WHAT WOULD WE BE MOVING INTO? WE DON'T KNOW WHAT HAS HAPPENED IN THE CITY.
PICT, RESHER ACTS OUT OF FEAR.
IT BLINDS HIM... MAKES HIM DESPERATE. WE CAN'T LET FEAR INFECT THE COLONY. IF WE PANIC OR TURN ON EACH OTHER, WE ARE DOOMED.
THAT'S WHY I NEED YOU HERE. WE MUST KEEP THE NESTS TOGETHER.
ALRIGHT, DAD. LET ME HELP YOU TO YOUR ROOM. ARE YOU SURE YOU ARE FEELING ALRIGHT?
YES, YES, I JUST NEED SOME REST.

MEANWHILE, NOT FAR AWAY...
HURRY!
WE HAVE TO MAKE IT TO THE DAM BEFORE NIGHTFALL.
CAW! CAW!
WHA--!?
CAW! CAW! CAW! CAW! CAW! CAW! CAW! CAW! CAW! CAW! CAW!
RAVENS. JUST RAVENS... NOTHING TO WORRY AB--
BEHIND YOU!!

GRRRRRR
GRRRRRRRRR
POOR FOOLS.
THEY WERE RECKLESS.
LOOK, SISTERS! IN THE TREES!
THE SHADOW HAS EYES IN THE FOREST, TOO. THEY MUST SEE FAR ON THOSE BLACK WINGS. WE ARE OUTMATCHED!
NONSENSE. THEY MAY SEE FAR, BUT THEY DO NOT SEE UP CLOSE. THEY CAN'T READ THE LEAVES AND VINES LIKE WE CAN.
THE VINES HAVE GROWN TANGLED. CONFUSED.
EVEN WE CAN'T MAKE THEM OUT NOW.
THEY HAVE SHOWN US ENOUGH. LET'S GO, SISTERS. THERE IS NOTHING FOR US TO DO HERE. WE MUST GET READY.

BACK AT THE COLONY, IN THE STOREROOM...
HEY, WIX! YOU'RE BACK!
HEY, MOTTLE.
WHAT'D YA GET ME?
GOOD TO SEE YOU, TOO.
HERE YOU GO, BRAT.
GIMME! GIMME!
BLEH! WHAT IS THIS SUPPOSED TO BE?
IT'S CHEESE. I THINK. OR MAYBE BREAD.
THIS IS GREEN AND FUZZY.
CHEESE ISN'T GREEN AND FUZZY. THIS IS ROTTEN.
IT'S AGED. THROW IT IN THE PILE IF YOU DON'T WANT IT. I'VE GOTTA CHECK US IN WITH PICT.
YUCK!
SO ARE YOU AND PICT GONNA GO MAKE OUT NOW?
DOUBLE YUCK.
SHUT IT, BRAT!
SMOOCHY, SMOOCHY, SMOOCH...
YOU THERE! WIX, RIGHT? PICT'S FRIEND?

OH, HELLO, KESSEL. YES. I'M WIX.
I HEAR YOU'RE ONE OF THE FASTEST SCAVENGERS IN THE COLONY.
FASTEST THERE IS!
GOOD! WE ARE HEADING OUT TO THE HIGHWAY TO CHECK OUT AN ABANDONED TRUCK THERE.
WE COULD USE A GOOD RUNNER IN CASE WE FIND SOMETHING. WOULD YOU LIKE TO JOIN US?
A TRUCK? I DON'T REMEMBER SEEING A TRUCK OUT THERE.
HMM... WELL IT'S PROBABLY FURTHER DOWN THAN YOU'VE BEEN. MOST LIKELY BLOCKED FROM VIEW BY THE FOREST.
THE... FOREST?
IS THAT A PROBLEM? OH, WHAT AM I SAYING! YOU JUST GOT IN. YOU MUST BE EXHAUSTED. I'LL--
NO! IT'S NO PROBLEM! WE'RE READY TO GO!
EXCELLENT! BUT--
WHERE WE GOING?

UMF, IS IT? YOU'RE FROM THE CITY, CORRECT?
YEAH?
I HAVE A DIFFERENT ASSIGNMENT FOR YOU. WE ARE SENDING MORE MICE TO THE CITY, AND WE NEED A STURDY RAT LIKE YOU TO GUIDE THEM. YOU LEAVE TOMORROW.
THE CITY?
UMF LOVES THE CITY! YOU CAN COUNT ON US, SIR!
EXCELLENT! GET SOME REST AND BE READY. WE LEAVE THIS EVENING.
WIX! THE CITY? I HATE THE CITY! THAT'S WHY I LEFT.
DON'T WORRY! YOU'LL BE FINE. THIS IS A CHANCE FOR US TO FINALLY GET OUT OF THIS DUMP!
NOW WE CAN FIND SOME REAL LOOT! WE'RE PRACTICALLY SCOUTS NOW! JUST WATCH WHAT YOU EAT AND I'LL SEE YOU WHEN WE GET BACK!
I GUESS SO...
GREAT, I GOTTA GO LET PICT KNOW WE'RE BACK. SEE YA LATER!

THE ATTIC...
-sigh-
SO MUCH FOR THE SUN...
WILL THIS RAIN EVER END?
HEY! WE'RE BACK.
IT TOOK YOU LONG ENOUGH.
EVERYONE ASSUMED YOU WERE CAT FOOD.
ME? CAT FOOD? STUPID CATS ARE NO TROUBLE FOR ME.
THAT'S NOT WHAT I HEARD. DID YOU AT LEAST BRING SOMETHING BACK THIS TIME?
IF YOU WANT ME TO BRING SOMETHING BACK, SEND ME TO A HOUSE WITH SOMETHING IN IT.
I WOULD IF THERE WERE ANY LEFT.
THAT'S ALRIGHT, PICT, I GOT A NEW ASSIGNMENT, STRAIGHT FROM KESSEL HIMSELF. I'M GOING ALL THE WAY OUT TO THE HIGHWAY TO--
WHAT!?
YOU'RE GOING!? WELL, THAT'S JUST GREAT! I JUST SIT HERE IN THIS MOLDY OLD HOUSE WHILE YOU GET TO GO PLAY IN THE WOODS!
HEY, SORRY, PICT, MAYBE YOU COULD COME WITH US IF I TALKED TO KESSEL ABOUT IT.
-sigh-
NO.
I HAVE TO STAY HERE AND MAKE SURE RESHER DOESN'T START A REVOLT OR SOMETHING.

THAT WINDBAG? I WOULDN'T WORRY ABOUT HIM.
DAD THINKS HE'S UP TO SOMETHING.
RESH STILL THINKS WE SHOULD GO TO THE CITY? IT'S NOT THE WORST IDEA I'VE EVER HEARD.
DO YOU THINK WE SHOULD? WHAT IF THE HUMANS AREN'T THERE?
IF IT'S AS BIG AS I'VE HEARD, I'M SURE THERE'S STILL SOME GOOD LOOT IN THERE.
MAYBE, BUT IF OTHER OUTLYING COLONIES HAVE THE SAME IDEA, THERE WILL BE EVEN MORE MOUTHS TO FEED, AND WHAT HAPPENS WHEN WE RUN OUT AGAIN?
WE HAVE TO DO SOMETHING SOON. WE HAVE TO GO SOMEWHERE. MAYBE IN THE FOREST--
THE FOREST AGAIN? IT'S NO PLACE FOR A MOUSE.
WHY NOT? WE WOULDN'T HAVE TO WORRY ABOUT POISONS, OR TRAPS.
AND THERE IS PLENTY OF FOOD... BERRIES! FRESH ONES! NOT THE ROTTEN ONES WE DIG OUT OF THE TRASH. AND--
AND *SNAKES!* AND OWLS. AND WHO KNOWS WHAT ELSE.
HAVE YOU BEEN? TO THE FOREST?
I SKIRTED AROUND THE EDGE A FEW TIMES TO AVOID THE CATS--THEY WON'T GO THERE EITHER...

"I ALWAYS FELT LIKE SOMETHING WAS WATCHING ME FROM IN THERE... AND THEN YESTERDAY...
"I THINK I SAW IT!"
"SAW WHAT?"
"I DON'T KNOW EXACTLY... A GREAT BEAST--BIGGER THAN A DOG--WITH HUGE FANGS AND COLD EYES."
HAHA! MAYBE IT WAS A DEER.
IT WAS NOT A DEER! IT WAS... SOMETHING ELSE.
WIX... BE CAREFUL OUT THERE. IT IS A LONG WAY AND KESSEL SAID IT MIGHT BE DANGEROUS.
DON'T WORRY ABOUT ME, PICT. I'LL BE OK.

LATER, IN THE BASEMENT...
SKEK...
ARE THEY BACK?
GOT BACK A FEW MINUTES AGO. THEY LOOK ANGRY.
GOOD. I WANT THEM ANGRY. IS EVERYTHING IN PLACE?
THE BOYS ARE ON IT NOW, BOSS. ARE YOU SURE ABOUT THIS?
THIS WILL ENSURE THE FUTURE OF THE COLONY, SKEK.
OF COURSE I'M SURE.
MEET ME BACK IN THE STOREROOM WHEN EVERYTHING IS READY.
SQUEAK SQUEAK
YES, BOSS.
ahem

MEEOWW

IDIOT.

TITAN! I HEARD A FUNNY STORY TODAY. IN FACT, IT'S QUITE POPULAR AROUND HERE THIS MORNING.

GO AWAY, RODENT.

I'M IN NO MOOD.

ALL THE MICE ARE LAUGHING ABOUT IT.

IT SEEMS YOU WERE ONCE AGAIN OUTWITTED BY THE RED MOUSE AND HIS OAFISH RAT FRIEND.

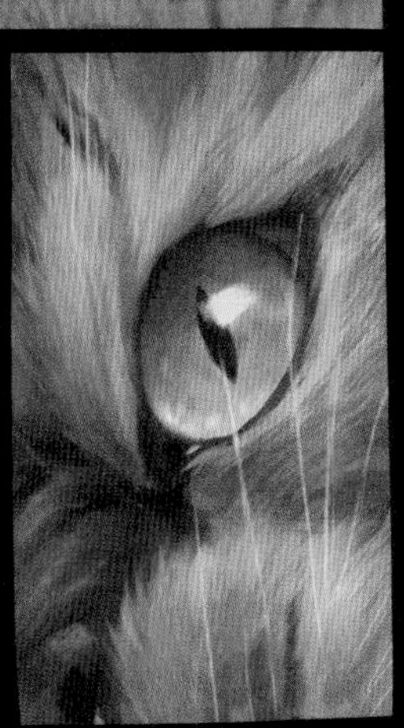

REEEOWRR!
WHAT DID YOU SAY!?

THAT'S TWICE NOW THAT HE'S MADE YOU LOOK STUPID, ISN'T IT?
GRRRRRRR
YOU FOOL! YOU THINK YOU'RE SAFE IN THERE, BUT WE WILL FIND A WAY IN!
AND WHEN WE DO, YOU WILL BE MY DINNER.

NOW, NOW, TITAN, I DIDN'T COME HERE TO TEASE YOU. I CAME HERE TO ***HELP*** YOU.
I DON'T NEED YOUR HELP. YOU ARE ***MEAT.***

HOW WOULD YOU LIKE ANOTHER CHANCE AT HIM? THINK YOU COULD FINISH THE JOB THIS TIME?
WHAT?

I HAPPEN TO KNOW EXACTLY WHERE HE WILL BE THIS EVENING...

ALONG WITH A FEW OTHERS...
THERE WILL BE PLENTY FOR ALL OF YOUR... HERD OR WHATEVER.
YOU WOULD SEND SO MANY OF YOUR OWN KIND TO THEIR DEATHS?
THIS IS A DISTRACTION ... OR A TRAP. WHY SHOULD I BELIEVE YOU?
TITAN, WHEN HAVE I EVER LIED TO YOU?
-sigh- LET'S MAKE THIS SIMPLE: YOUR USUAL REWARD-- PLUS AN EXTRA PACK--WILL BE WAITING FOR YOU WHEN IT'S DONE.
KITTY KRACK
PREMIUM CATNIP
NIP? TWO PACKS!? GIVE! GIVE IT!
YOU WILL GET THEM AFTER THE JOB IS DONE! I DON'T WANT YOU STUMBLING AROUND SPOOKING THEM AWAY.

GIVE US A TASTE... AS A TOKEN OF GOOD WILL.

YESSSSSS... NO SURVIVORS!

ELSEWHERE...
SNIFF
SNIFF
SNIFF
SNIFF

LATER, IN THE STORE-ROOM, WIX PREPARES TO LEAVE...
DO TRY NOT TO GET EATEN, WIX.
YEAH, YEAH.
I GOT A BAD FEELING ABOUT SPLITTING UP LIKE THIS.
DON'T WORRY, UMF. IT'S ONLY TEMPORARY. JUST STAY ALERT ON THE WAY TO THE CITY, AND WE'LL BE DIGGING UP LOOT TOGETHER AGAIN IN NO TIME.
WIX, LET'S GO. TAKE THE LEAD UNTIL WE GET TO THE WOODS.
YES, SIR!
SEE YA LATER, GUYS!
KESSEL, PLEASE KEEP AN EYE ON HIM. HE GETS AHEAD OF HIMSELF SOMETIMES.
YOU REALLY CARE ABOUT HIM, DON'T YOU?
WELL... YES, WE GREW UP TOGETHER. EVER SINCE DAD FOUND HIM OUTSIDE THE HOUSE.
FOR YOU, I WILL DO MY BEST.
THANK YOU.
I SHOULD GO CHECK ON MY FATHER NOW...
I'M AFRAID HE MAY BE GETTING ILL.
OH? THAT'S TERRIBLE! HE IS LUCKY TO HAVE A DAUGHTER LIKE YOU THEN.
HE'S A TOUGH OLD MOUSE. I'M SURE HE'LL BE FINE.
YES... WELL... GOOD LUCK TO YOU, KESS. BE CAREFUL.

ORIM'S CHAMBER...
ZZZ... KOFF! KOFF!
ZZZ...
LOOKS LIKE HE'S FINALLY ASLEEP.
-sigh- HE'S GETTING WORSE...
MAYBE I CAN FIND SOMETHING IN THE STORE ROOM TO HELP.
HAVE KESSEL AND HIS SCOUTS LEFT YET?
HUH?
YES, BOSS.
IS EVERYTHING READY?
THE CATS ARE IN POSITION. WE GAVE THEM SOME NIP LIKE YOU SAID AND BLOCKED OFF THE ESCAPE ROUTES.
CATS?
GOOD, HOPEFULLY THE FOOLS WON'T SPRING THE TRAP TOO EARLY...
THE RED ONE HAS A NOSE FOR TRAPS.
ONCE THEY ARE IN THE OPEN, IT WON'T MATTER. THE CATS WILL MAKE SHORT WORK OF THEM.
NO!

I HAVE TO WARN THEM!
SMACK!
≈gasp!≈
CRASH
BAM!
BONG!
EH?
SOMEONE'S HERE!
PICT!?
GET HER!
RESHER! WHAT HAVE YOU DONE!?
DON'T LET HER GET AWAY!

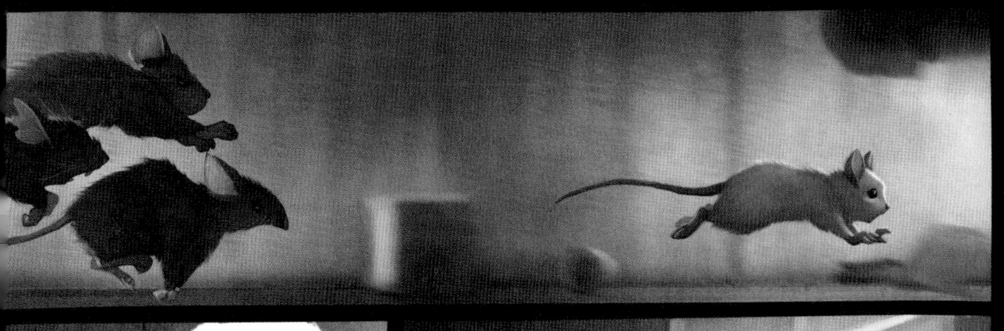

I HAVE TO GET OUT OF HERE!

THE WINDOW!

HURRY!
SHE'S ESCAPING!

SHE'S TRYING TO WARN THEM.

LET HER GO. SHE'S TOO LATE.

IF SHE DOES RETURN...
KILL HER.

PART III
GRIM SHADOWS

I HAVE TO FIND THEM BEFORE IT'S TOO LATE!
WHERE ARE THEY?
KESSEL!
HE'S HURT!

KESSEL! ARE YOU OK?
PICT!?
WHY ARE YOU HERE! GO BACK-AAGH!!
YOU'RE HURT.
I'LL BE ALRIGHT... I JUST NEED TO REST A MOMENT.
WE WERE AMBUSHED... BY THE CATS.
WHAT? HOW DO YOU KNO-- ERRGH!!
IT WAS RESHER! HE SENT THEM!

PICT, NO!
REEEEEOWRR!!!
WAIT HERE.

≈gasp!≈

NOTHING I CAN DO FOR THEM NOW.
I HAVE TO FIND WIX!

WHERE IS--
BEHIND YOU!
HUH?
EEEP!
CHOMP!!

RARRR!!!
SCRATCH!
SCRATCH!
HHSSSSSSSSSSSSS...

PICT? WHAT'S SHE DOING UP THERE?
UMM...
UH-OH.
?
NO!
COME BACK HERE, YOU STUPID CAT!
SWIPE
WOAH!
HELLO AGAIN!

PRETTY
MOUSE...

EH?

OH
NO.

AAAWEEERRRK!

NO!
MINE!
CREEEAK
RUMBLE
CRASH!

OOPH!

HSSSSSS...

FWOOOOM
THWAK!

HUH.

UH-OH.
SHE'S TRAPPED!

WOOOSH

IT'S GONNA FLY OFF WITH HER!
GOTTA GET HER OUT OF THERE!
SKREEEEAAH

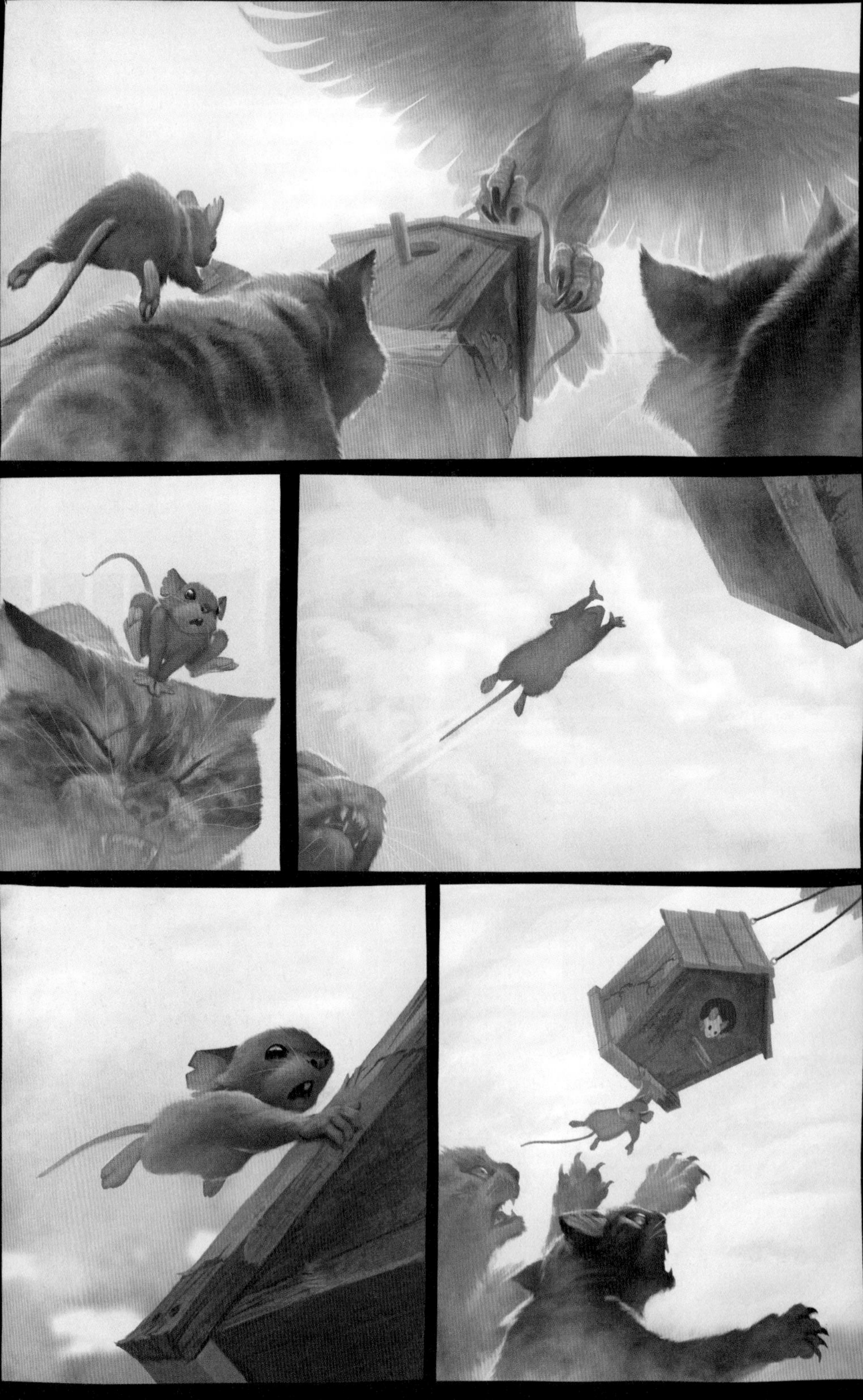

WIX!
HANG ON!
NO!
CRACK
WIX!
oooph!
SPLASH

OUCH.
PICT!
UH-OH.

THE FOREST! IT'S MY ONLY HOPE!
BUT WHAT ABOUT THE BEAST?
NO CHOICE NOW...
HE ESCAPED!

GO!
AFTER HIM!

N-NO...
NOT IN THERE!

GRRR...

NO.
NOT THIS TIME!

RAARRRRR!

GRRRRR
MEEOWWwrr!
SNAP!

HUH?
I THOUGHT HE HAD ME...

gasp

I THINK THAT'S MY CUE TO LEAVE!

WHAT'S THIS?

SNIFF
SNIFF

ANOTHER USURPER IN MY WOODS?
HAVE YOU ALSO COME TO CHALLENGE ME FOR MY KINGDOM?
HAHAHAHAHAH
NO, JUST A LITTLE MOUSE, TOO FAR FROM HOME.
SUCH A PITIFUL LITTLE CREATURE... SO WEAK AND POWERLESS... WITH NO IDEA WHAT HAS HAPPENED.
PERHAPS I SHOULD ENVY YOU.
GO BACK TO YOUR HUMANS, LITTLE MOUSE. WAIT FOR THE END. IT COMES SOON ENOUGH.

BUT NO... THEY ARE GONE NOW, AREN'T THEY?

YOU SEE, I'VE BEEN WATCHING...

I WATCH THE MICE...

I WATCH THE CATS...

I WATCH AND I WATCH, BUT I SEE NO HUMANS.

PICT...
I CAN'T GO BACK NOW.
SEE YOU SOON.

PART IV

HAWKRIDER

WHERE...

WOAH!

THIS
IS NOT
GOOD.

WHERE IS SHE TAKING ME?

I WON'T BE BIRD FOOD...

I'D RATHER TAKE MY CHANCES DOWN THERE. I THINK I SEE WATER... MAYBE I CAN...

WAIT. IS THAT A--

ACK!!!
CAW! CAW!

KRRAAAH!
oopH

CAW!
CAW!
KRAAAHH

KRAAAHK!
SKREEEEAH!!!

I GOTTA GET OUT OF HERE!

RAAA
AAAYEEEE!!!
SPLASH!
gasp!

WHAT HAPPENED HERE?
WOAH!
SPLOOSH

EW.

THUD

IT'S FREEZING. I HAVE TO FIND SHELTER.

pssst
BETTER HIDE, MOUSE.

SHE HASN'T GIVEN UP ON YOU YET.

OVER HERE. HURRY!

COME. COME. STAY UNDER THE FOLIAGE WHERE YOU CAN.
YOU WON'T LAST LONG OUT IN THE OPEN WITH THAT FUR.
YOU'RE A LUCKY ONE, YOU KNOW THAT?
A WEEK AGO THAT WATER WAS FROZEN SOLID.
WOULDN'T HAVE BEEN SUCH A SOFT LANDING THEN, EH?
N-NO...I SUPPOSE NOT.
A HAWK HAD ME...
BUT WE WERE ATTACKED...
BY RAVENS.
YEP, RAVENS ALL OVER THESE PARTS.
spit!
DON'T TRUST ANY OF 'EM! NOTHING BUT OILY SNAKES WITH WINGS!
THEY PROBABLY JUST WANTED YOU TO THEMSELVES.
NAME'S SNAG, BY THE WAY.
OH, I'M PICT. NICE TO MEET YOU.
THIS WAY, MS. PICT.

WHERE ARE WE GOING?
MY PLACE. FINEST TREE ON THE WHOLE ISLAND.
hmph! NOT SAYING MUCH.
ISLAND?
YEP. THE "REFUGE" THEY CALL IT.
hmph! NOTHING BUT A HILL OF MUD!
YOU CAN REST HERE TONIGHT. THAT CUT WILL NEED TO BE LOOKED AFTER.
I CAN'T STAY HERE. I HAVE TO GET HOME!
SORRY, MS. MOUSE. UNLESS YOU GOT WINGS, THERE AIN'T NO GETTING OFF THE ISLAND...
...NOT UNTIL TOMORROW ANYWAYS.
BUT MY FATHER'S IN TROUBLE! AND WIX...
...WHAT HAPPENED TO WIX?
AND DON'T THINK ABOUT SWIMMING FOR IT EITHER! YOU WON'T LAST FIVE MINUTES IN THAT FRIGID WATER.
A FROZEN MOUSE IS NO GOOD TO ANYONE.

IN THE MORNING WE'LL HEAD TO THE CAMP..
THE BEAVERS WILL BE THERE. THEY CAN FERRY YOU ACROSS IF YOU STILL WANT TO GO.
NOT SURE IF YOU WANT TO CROSS BACK, THOUGH.
NOT WITH ALL THOSE WOLVES ABOUT.
WOLVES?
WHAT'S A WOLV?
HA! "WOLV."
NOT FROM AROUND HERE I TAKE IT?
NO, I'M FROM SOUTH OF HERE, IN THE HUMAN HOUSES. DO YOU KNOW THEM?
HUMANS?
Hmph!
NEVER BEEN AROUND 'EM MYSELF, BUT I KNOW SOME SQUIRRELS FROM AROUND THERE.
IT'S A FEW DAYS WALK I THINK.
A FEW DAYS?! BUT THAT'S SO FAR AWAY...
WELL, YOU COULD TRY HITCHING A RIDE BACK WITH THAT HAWK, BUT I WOULDN'T RECOMMEND IT.
AH, SORRY. JUST A JOKE THERE...
I KNOW YOU'RE IN A HURRY, BUT THERE'S NOWHERE TO GO FOR NOW.
IT WILL BE DARK SOON, ANYWAY.
TOMORROW YOU CAN GET STARTED. BEST TO REST UP UNTIL THE MORNING.

ELSEWHERE...
WHICH WAY?
I THINK IT FLEW IN THIS DIRECTION...

EH?
RUMBLE
GET OFF!
WHO BOTHERS SKOGA?!
EEP!

SORRY, I... UH... I THOUGHT YOU WERE A ROCK! UM, YOU DON'T EAT MICE, DO YOU?
BLECH! NO, TOO MUCH HAIR. BUT IF YOU KEEP BOTHERING SKOGA, HE WILL MAKE AN EXCEPTION!
I'M REALLY SORRY TO BOTHER YOU, BUT I THINK I'M LOST. I'M LOOKING FOR A HAWK. IT FLEW THIS WAY... I THINK...
HAVE YOU SEEN IT?
A HAWK?

A *MOUSE* LOOKING FOR A *HAWK?!*
IF YOU WANT TO DIE, JUST DROWN YOURSELF IN THE STREAM...
AND DO IT QUIETLY!
NO, THAT'S NOT--I JUST NEED TO FIND IT!
DO YOU KNOW WHERE THE HAWK LIVES OR NOT?

"THAT BIRD DOESN'T LIVE IN THESE WOODS.
"SHE LIVES MILES AWAY, ON THE MOUNTAIN, BEYOND THE TOWN, PAST THE LAKE."
MOUNTAIN?
IS IT FAR? HOW LONG WILL IT TAKE ME TO GET THERE?
HOHAHAH! YOU?! GET THERE?
IT WOULD TAKE DOZENS OF YOUR LIFETIMES TO GET THERE. THERE IS NO WAY.
GO HOME, FOOLISH MOUSE.
NO!
THERE MUST BE SOME WAY TO GET THERE!
AAAARRROOOOOO
EH?
THAT SOUND...
YOU BRING DEATH WITH YOU...
WHAT?
DEATH? YOU MEAN THE BEASTS! WHAT ARE THEY?
SCOURERS...
DEVOURERS.
...OF EVERYTHING.
THE EASTERN WOODS HAVE GROWN QUIET...
AND NOW THEY COME HERE!

WHAT DO WE DO?
WE? YOU WILL DIE, AS ALL MICE DO.
THAT IS THE NATURE OF MICE.
IT IS SKOGA'S NATURE TO WAIT, SO HE WILL.
KINGS AND TYRANTS COME AND GO...
...EVEN HUMANS COME AND GO...
BUT SKOGA LASTS. SKOGA WILL WAIT.
I CAN'T JUST WAIT!
NO, YOU CANNOT. MICE DO NOT WAIT.
WELL, YOU'RE NO HELP!
NO.
SKOGA IS NO HELP.
FINE, WHO NEEDS A STUPID TURTLE?
I'LL FIND HER MYSELF.

THE NEXT MORNING, PICT AND SNAG PREPARE TO HEAD TO THE CAMP...
YOU SLEEP OK? HOW'S THE ARM?
IT'S A LITTLE SORE, BUT I'LL BE FINE, THANKS.
GOOD, WE BETTER GET GOING. IT LOOKS LIKE MORE RAIN IS COMING.
SO EVERYONE IS ON THIS ISLAND NOW?
MOSTLY.
IT'S THE ONLY PLACE AROUND THAT ISN'T FLOODED OR CRAWLING WITH WOLVES.
HOW DID IT ALL GET THIS WAY?
WELL, I DON'T KNOW ABOUT ALL THIS HUMAN TRASH LAYING AROUND...
BUT AS FOR THE WATER, YOU CAN THANK OUR GLORIOUS BEAVER OVERLORDS FOR THAT!
BEAVERS DID THIS?
HMPH! I'M NOT SURE WHO'S WORSE: THE WOLVES OR THOSE FLAT-TAILED FOOLS.
"YOU SEE, WHEN THE WOLVES CAME AND STARTED HUNTING US DAY AND NIGHT, NONE OF US KNEW WHAT TO DO. MOST OF US HAD NEVER EVEN SEEN A WOLF BEFORE.
"THEN THE BEAVERS CAME DOWN RIVER. THEY CLAIMED THE WHOLE FOREST FOR THEIR FOOL KING, AND SAID THEY WOULD PROTECT US IN RETURN FOR HELP WORKING ON THEIR DAM. I SAID WE DIDN'T NEED THEIR HELP, BUT MOST WERE AFRAID OF THE WOLVES, SO THEY AGREED TO WORK.

"THEY DAMMED UP THE WHOLE PLACE TO KEEP THE WOLVES OUT.
"hmph! SOME PLAN! MY TREE IS OUT IN THE LAKE NOW!"
THEN THEY MOVED US OUT HERE TO THIS HEAP FOR "PROTECTION," AND HERE WE SIT.
NOTHING TO DO. NOTHING TO EAT, AND WE CAN'T EVEN LEAVE WITHOUT THE BEAVERS' SAY SO.
WE'D BE BETTER OFF WITH THE WOLVES IF YOU ASK ME.
THIS WAY, MS. MOUSE. THE CAMP IS UP AHEAD.

EH? WHO'S THAT OUT THERE?
IT'S SNAG, YOU OLD VARMINT! I BROUGHT AN OUTSIDER. SAYS SHE WANTS TO FLOAT ACROSS WITH THE BEAVERS. ANY AROUND?
FLOAT BACK? WHY SHE WANT TO DO A FOOL THING LIKE THAT?
SHE HAS HER REASONS. ANY BEAVERS AROUND OR NOT?
YEAH, THAT ENGINEER OF THEIRS SHOWED UP A MINUTE AGO LOOKING FOR MORE WORKERS.
THE YELLING HAS ALREADY STARTED. JUST HEAD TOWARD THE COMMOTION.
OH GREAT.
LISTEN UP!
THERE WAS A SMALL BREACH ON THE WESTERN SIDE OF THE DAM. WE WILL REQUIRE MORE WORKERS TO--
NO! NO MORE HELP WITHOUT FOOD!
WE JUST NEED A LITTLE MORE HELP SECURING THE BASE AND PATCHING UP SOME HOLES.
LIES!
IT'S TOO BIG ALREADY! IF THAT DAM GETS ANY HIGHER, WE'LL BE FLOODED OFF THE ISLAND!
I ALREADY HAD TO MOVE OUT OF MY HOLE!
THAT ONE'S CALLED ARKEN. BEAVERS CALL HIM THE "MASTER ENGINEER."
HE'S THE ONE TO TALK TO IF YOU WANT OFF THE ISLAND.

WHEN WILL YOU SEND OUT MORE FORAGERS, ARKEN?
HOW MUCH FOOD ARE YOU KEEPING FOR *YOURSELVES?*
WHAT? NOTHING! LOOK, WE'RE ALL HUNGRY, BUT THE DAM IS THE PRIORITY! THERE WILL BE MORE TIME FOR FORAGING WHEN THE WORK IS COMPLETED.
IT WILL NEVER BE COMPLETED! YOUR KING HAS GONE MAD!
BE QUIET, MARMOT! THE KING PROTECTS YOU!
EASY, FRIENDS.
UM... EXCUSE ME...
MY NAME IS PICT. I AM FROM SOUTH OF HERE...

YOU MADE IT ALL THE WAY UP HERE FROM THE SOUTH? I SERIOUSLY DOUBT THAT!
IT'S TRUE! I FISHED HER OUT OF THE SOUTH SIDE OF THE LAKE YESTERDAY.
DID YOU SEE THE WOLVES? HOW MANY WERE THERE? ARE THEY COMING HERE?
WE LIVE IN THE HUMAN DWELLINGS. I HAVEN'T SEEN ANY WOLVES. I WAS--
HAVEN'T SEEN ANY?! THEN WHERE ARE THOSE WHO WENT TO THE CAVE? WHY DIDN'T THEY COME BACK?
SHE'S PROBABLY A SPY FOR THE WOLVES!
SHE'S NOT A SPY, FRAG, YOU OLD FOOL!
EVERYONE CALM DOWN. LET HER SPEAK.
THERE ARE MANY OF US STILL LIVING THERE, BUT WE ARE RUNNING OUT OF FOOD AND MAY HAVE TO LEAVE SOON.
WE WOULD BE HAPPY TO HELP YOU FIND FOOD IN RETURN FOR PROTECTION HERE ON THE ISLAND, IF THE WOODS ARE REALLY SO DANGEROUS.

THERE ARE TOO MANY HERE ALREADY. WE HAVE ENOUGH MOUTHS TO FEED.
WE ARE SMALL AND DON'T NEED MUCH.
AND IF THERE IS FOOD TO BE FOUND, MY SCAVENGERS WILL FIND IT! WE CAN WORK ON THE DAM, TOO.
HMM...TOO SMALL FOR GATHERING WOOD...
BUT I SUPPOSE WE CAN ALWAYS USE MORE MUD PATTERS AT THE BASE. IT CAN BE HARD, DANGEROUS WORK, THOUGH.
WE CAN DO IT! BUT FIRST I HAVE TO GET OFF THIS ISLAND AND BACK HOME.
VERY WELL. OUR KING WILL HAVE TO AGREE TO MORE REFUGEES, BUT I WILL TAKE YOU TO HIM.
FETCH THE RAFT.
YES, SIR.
ANYONE WHO CAN WORK MUST COME WITH US!
FULL RATIONS FOR THOSE WHO WORK!
BAH! I'LL GO. IT'S BORING HERE ANYWAY.

THE COLONY HOUSE...
WHERE IS HE? HE SHOULD HAVE BEEN BACK BY NOW.
GET THE BOYS AND GO OUT AGAIN...
I WANT HIM FOUND!
YES, BOSS.
OH, THERE YOU ARE. WHAT TOOK YOU SO LONG?
SORRY I'M LATE, RESHER...
...BUT YOUR CATS NEARLY GOT ME KILLED!
KESSEL! I DON'T--
I SHOULD KILL YOU RIGHT NOW!

EASY, KESSEL, EASY... THE CATS ARE WILD BEASTS, I DON'T HAVE THAT KIND OF CONTROL OVER THEM.
I CAN ONLY POINT THEM IN THE RIGHT DIRECTION.
BESIDES...
...YOU WERE SUPPOSED TO GET OUT OF THEIR WAY!
I TRIED.
THEY ARE MORE CUNNING THAN THEY LOOK. ONE WAS WAITING FOR ME ON MY WAY BACK. HE NEARLY HAD MY HEAD.
I HAD TO HIDE FOR HOURS UNTIL I COULD RETURN.
KESSEL, I'M JUST GLAD YOU MADE IT BACK.
WE WERE BEGINNING TO WORRY.
SURE YOU WERE.

IS IT DONE?
THE OTHERS ARE...?
THEY WON'T BE IN OUR WAY.
I ACCOUNTED FOR ALL BUT ONE BODY, AND I DON'T EXPECT HIM TO RETURN.
THERE IS SOMETHING ELSE...
PICT WAS THERE.
I... I BELIEVE SHE PERISHED AS WELL.
WHAT? THAT IS JUST AWFUL! WHAT A **TRAGEDY**! I KNOW YOU WERE FOND OF HER.
SHE KNEW ABOUT YOUR PLAN. ANY IDEA HOW THAT HAPPENED?
OH? I HAVE NO IDEA! BUT SHE WAS ALWAYS SNOOPING AROUND.
PERHAPS SHE HEARD ONE OF OUR MICE TALKING.
THEY CAN BE SUCH BLABBER-MOUTHS.
HER IDEAS WERE AS FOOLISH AS THE ELDERS' INACTION...
BUT THAT WASN'T PART OF THE PLAN.
WHAT'S DONE IS DONE. YOU KNEW THERE WOULD BE RISKS.
BUT THIS IS FOR THE GOOD OF THE COLONY.
ONCE WE'RE IN THE CITY, WE CAN PUT THIS BEHIND US.
GET THOSE CUTS LOOKED AFTER, WE HAVE TO INFORM THE ELDERS THAT THEIR LAST HOPE FOR STAYING HAS FAILED.

PART V

KINGS OF MADNESS

SOMEWHERE...

CREEEEK
HUH?

CLICK-*
NO...

TITAN?!
RRRRED MOUSE...

YOU ARE LOST.

YOU'LL NEVER FIND HER, YOU KNOW.
THAT OLD TURTLE WAS RIGHT. YOU ARE JUST A MOUSE...
AND MICE WERE MADE TO DIE.
NO! I BEAT YOU, DIDN'T I?
YOU WERE LUCKY!
BUT YOU'LL NEED MORE THAN LUCK...
TO SURVIVE WHAT'S COMING!

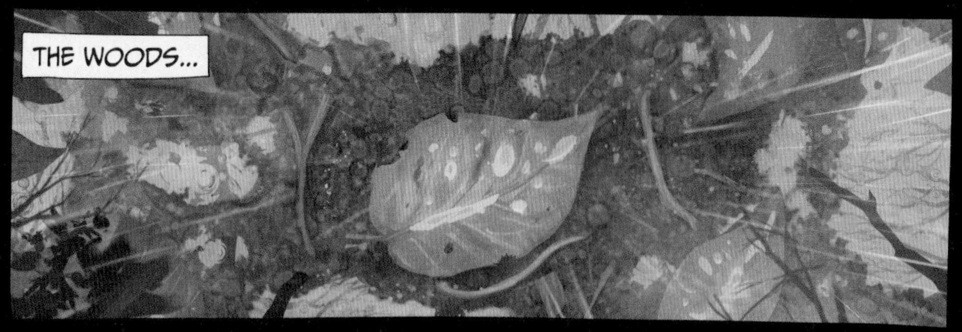
THE WOODS...

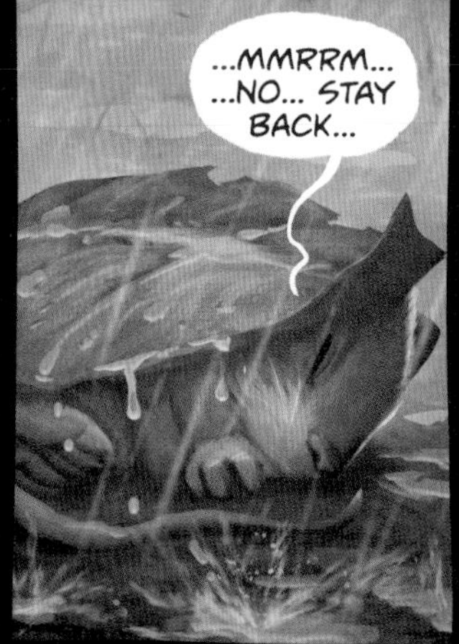
...MMRRM...
...NO... STAY BACK...

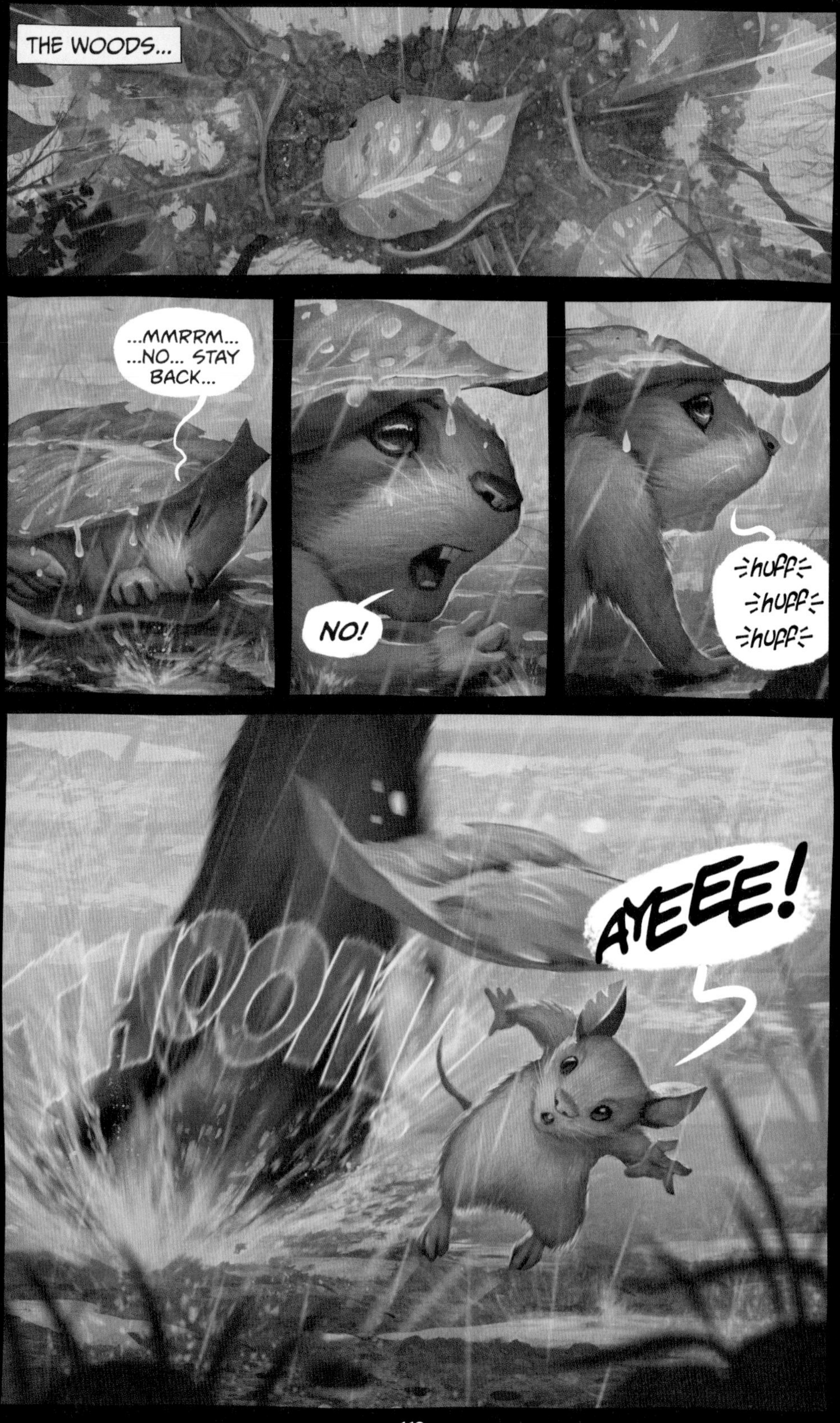

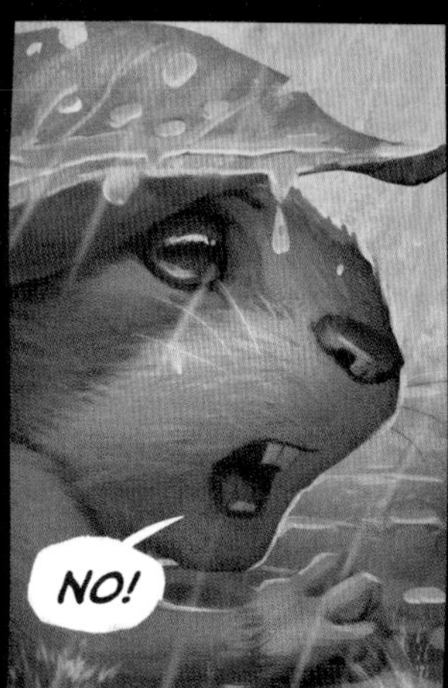
NO!

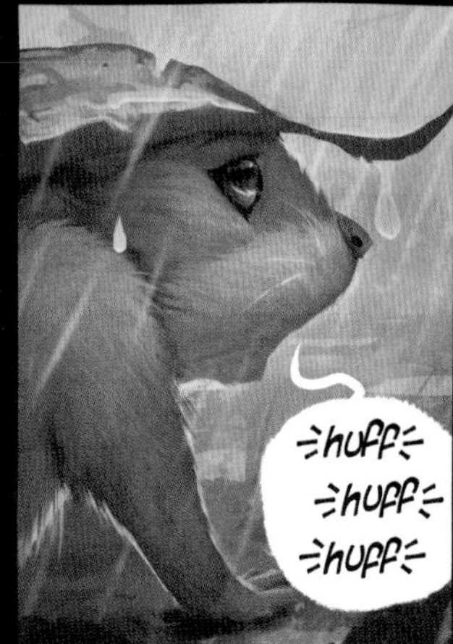
huff
huff
huff

AYEEE!

THOOM!
AAAAH!!!
SPLASH!
OH, SORRY ABOUT THAT!
DIDN'T SEE YOU THERE...
SPLASH!
...BUT YOU REALLY SHOULDN'T SLEEP OUT IN THE OPEN LIKE THAT.
COME OUT OF THERE. I WON'T HURT YOU.

Y-YOU WON'T EAT ME?
EAT YOU?
HA! NO OFFENSE, BUT YOU DON'T LOOK THAT TASTY TO ME.
THE NAME'S ATLAS. HOW ARE YA?
OH. I'M WIX. I...I THINK I'M LOST.
YOU SEE, I WAS LOOKING FOR MY FRIEND, SHE WAS GRABBED BY A HAWK...
...AND THEN THIS STUPID OLD TURTLE TOLD ME SHE WAS TAKEN TO A MOUNTAIN, BUT THEN--
TURTLE? HAWK? LISTEN, I HATE TO TELL YOU THIS, BUT IF YOUR FRIEND WAS TAKEN BY A HAWK... WELL...
NO! YOU DON'T UNDERSTAND! THE HAWK CAN'T GET TO HER.
SHE WAS IN A BIRDHOUSE. I JUST HAVE TO FIND HER BEFORE IT CAN GET INSIDE.
HMM... WELL, THE ONLY MOUNTAIN I KNOW IS A LONG WAY FROM HERE.
WHICH WAY?!

LISTEN, YOU'LL NEVER GET THERE ON THOSE STUBBY LEGS, BUT I'M HEADED THAT WAY... TO SOME PLACE CALLED "THE REFUGE."
HAVE YOU HEARD OF IT?
NO. I'M NOT FROM AROUND HERE.
HEH, I FIGURED. ME NEITHER.
TELL YOU WHAT, I'LL GIVE YOU A LIFT THERE. THEN YOU CAN DECIDE IF YOU WANT TO KEEP GOING.
WHAT'S THE CATCH?
NO CATCH. TO BE HONEST, I COULD USE THE COMPANY. THESE WOODS ARE SO QUIET.
I HAVEN'T SEEN ANY OTHER CRITTERS AROUND.
THESE WOODS DO SEEM MOSTLY EMPTY, NOW THAT YOU MENTION IT.
HOP ON UP, WE'VE GOT A LOT OF GROUND TO COVER, AND I HAVE TO MAKE A STOP ON THE WAY.
WELL... OK.
READY?
I THINK SO.
OK. HANG ON.
AND IF YOU GET THE URGE TO SCRATCH BEHIND THOSE EARS, I'D REALLY APPRECIATE IT.

THANKS FOR THE RIDE. IS IT FAR?
IT'S A GOOD DISTANCE, BUT WE CAN PROBABLY MAKE IT BEFORE NIGHTFALL.
GOOD. I WANT TO GET THERE AND GET OUT OF THESE WOODS AS SOON AS POSSIBLE.
OH? THIS PLACE DOESN'T SEEM SO BAD. UNLIKE MY OLD WOODS, THERE ARE STILL SOME PLANTS GROWING HERE...
EVEN IF THEY ARE A BIT WILTED.
NOT SO BAD? EASY FOR YOU TO SAY! YOU'RE ***HUGE!*** NOTHING WILL MESS WITH YOU OUT HERE. THIS IS NO PLACE FOR A MOUSE.
HAHAH! I SUPPOSE SO, BUT MICE ARE PRETTY TOUGH, TOO.
SOME OF THE TOUGHEST CRITTERS I KNOW ARE MICE. THESE WOODS ARE PROBABLY FULL OF THEM.
I DOUBT THAT, ATLAS.

IS IT ALWAYS COLD AND WET WHERE YOU'RE FROM, TOO, ATLAS?
YEP.
SNAP!
UGH! WELL, I HOPE THE WEATHER CHANGES SOON.
IT SHOULD HAVE ALREADY CHANGED. MY ANTLERS CAME IN WEEKS AGO.
OR WAS IT MONTHS?
WHO CAN KEEP TIME ANYMORE?
ANTLERS?
THOSE SPIKY THINGS YOU'RE SITTING BETWEEN.
OOHHHH. THAT'S WHAT THOSE ARE.

THE LAKE...

WORRIED ABOUT HAWKS?

Y-YES, A BIT.

NO NEED.

WE HAVE TALONS OF OUR OWN.

YES, AND OURS ARE LONGER, AS MANY A RAPTOR HAS FOUND OUT.

AH, HERE WE ARE...

WELCOME TO THE *LODGE!*

RAVENS!

DON'T WORRY ABOUT THEM...

THEY WON'T HARM YOU. THE KING MADE A DEAL WITH THEM.

THEY SERVE AS OUR EYES IN THE FOREST AND WARN US OF PREDATORS.

UMM... IF YOU SAY SO...

BUT THEY DIDN'T SEEM FRIENDLY BEFORE.

THEY WERE PROBABLY JUST TRYING TO DRIVE OFF THE HAWK. I'M SURE THAT WAS IT.

hmph! I DOUBT THAT VERY MUCH!

GET THE OTHERS TO THE DAM. I WILL JOIN YOU SOON.
WE WILL NEED TO INSPECT THE WESTERN WALL AGAIN. THERE HAVE BEEN MORE LEAKS.
WHAT? HOW COULD THAT BE? WE REINFORCED THAT AREA JUST A FEW DAYS AGO!
I DON'T KNOW. BUT WE HAVE TO FIND OUT.
hhhrgh!

THIS WAY, PICT.
SEE YA LATER, MS. MOUSE! COME SAY GOODBYE BEFORE YOU LEAVE!
I WILL, SNAG, AND THANKS FOR YOUR HELP!
...TRICKLING...
...I STILL HEAR IT...
UH-OH...
IS THAT THE KING?
THE TRICKLING!
SOUNDS LIKE HE'S IN ONE OF HIS...MOODS.
HELLO, ARKEN. GO RIGHT IN. HE'S BEEN LOOKING FOR YOU.
...DRIPPING...
...BABBLING...
I HEAR IT IN MY SLEEP!
...IT GROWS LOUDER!
I CAN HEAR IT EVEN NOW!

ARKEN!
ARKEN! THERE YOU ARE! THE TRICKLING! I STILL HEAR THE TRICKLING!
WHY IS MY DAM TRICKLING!?
YES... WELL...THERE WERE A FEW LEAKS--
LEAKS!?
I DON'T WANT TO HEAR ABOUT LEAKS! YOU SHOULD HAVE FILLED THOSE IN ALREADY!
IT'S A MINOR SETBACK I ASSURE YOU...
BUT MY KING...
PERHAPS BUILDING THE DAM HIGHER WHEN THERE HAS BEEN SO MUCH RAIN...
AGAIN HE QUESTIONS YOUR VISION, MY KING.
ARKEN, THE DAM MUST GO HIGHER! I DON'T WANT TO HEAR ANY MORE EXCUSES!
ARE YOU UP TO THIS? OR DO I HAVE TO FIND AN ENGINEER WHO IS?
YOU WILL HAVE YOUR DAM, MY KING. WE WILL REDOUBLE OUR EFFORTS.
SEE THAT YOU DO!
NOW, WHO IS THIS? WHO ARE YOU? SPEAK UP!
OH... UM...HELLO, UH, YOUR HIGHNESS...
MY NAME IS PICT, I REPRESENT A COLONY OF MICE DOWNSTREAM FROM HERE.

OH? COME HERE TO COMPLAIN ABOUT THE LACK OF WATER DOWNSTREAM, EH?
NO, GOOD KING, WE HAVE PLENTY OF WATER, BUT WE LACK FOOD. PERHAPS OUR TWO GROUPS COULD WORK TOGETHER TO FIND MORE, AND WE CAN HELP WITH THE DAM. TOGETHER WE--
WE DON'T HAVE FOOD FOR USELESS MICE.
AND WE DON'T NEED ANY MORE WORKERS.
YOU DON'T KNOW HOW MANY WORKERS WE NEED, NYLL!
AND UNLESS THE KING PUT YOU IN CHARGE OF BUILDING THE DAM, *I'M* STILL HEAD ENGINEER!
MY KING, IF WE ARE TO COMPLETE THE DAM QUICKLY, WE'LL NEED MORE PAWS.
PICT HERE ASSURES ME HER MICE AND RATS CAN HELP AND THEY DON'T REQUIRE MUCH FOOD.
RATS, TOO!? -*blech!*-
BUILD MY DAM MORE QUICKLY, YOU SAY?

YES! ARKEN! WE NEED MORE WORKERS!
YES. THE DAM MUST BE BUILT HIGHER! THE TRICKLING MUST STOP!
WELL, WE ARE HAPPY TO HELP! BUT--
VERY WELL, MOUSE, BRING YOUR REFUGEES TO THE ISLAND...
AND THOSE ABLE TO WORK MUST START WORKING IMMEDIATELY!
MY KING, I--
THAT IS ALL.
I CAN HEAR THAT INFERNAL TRICKLING FROM HERE. I CAN'T STAND IT! SEE THAT IT IS STOPPED, ARKEN! USE ALL THE WORKERS YOU CAN FIND!
YES, MY LORD.

MEANWHILE...
UGH... ROADS...
WE BETTER HURRY ACROSS.
WAIT A MINUTE...
I KNOW THIS PLACE.
WIX, THE ROADS ARE NOT SAFE--
THE HIGHWAY...
YES, THAT'S THE OVERPASS OVER THERE! THIS IS THE PLACE!
THIS IS WHERE WE WERE GOING BEFORE WE WERE AMBUSHED BY THE CATS! WE'RE HERE!
BUT WHERE'S...
WHERE'S WHAT?

IT'S NOT HERE...
WHAT'S NOT HERE?
THE TRUCK! IT'S LIKE ONE OF THESE, BUT MUCH BIGGER, AND THEY HAVE FOOD IN THEM SOMETIMES!
WE WERE SENT HERE TO FIND IT.
BUT IT'S NOT HERE...
MAYBE SOMETHING MOVED IT.
NO, THAT'S IMPOSSIBLE.
EVEN YOU COULDN'T MOVE IT. ONLY THE HUMANS COULD DO THAT, AND THEY'RE GONE. IT...
IT WAS NEVER HERE.
SNIFF SNIFF HMM...
WHAT IS IT?

WIX,
TO ME!
NOW!
I
DON'T SEE
ANYTHING.
WAIT...
WOLVES!

BETTER RUN, MOOSE.
I'M FINE RIGHT HERE, WOLF.

GRRRR
RRR
RRRR
GRRRRRRRR

ATLAS...
YOU'RE A LONG WAY FROM HOME.

THESE AREN'T YOUR WOODS.

I COULD SAY THE SAME TO YOU, ***EREBUS.***
OH? BUT THESE ARE MY WOODS. I HAVE CLAIMED THEM.
ALL OF THIS IS MINE NOW.
EVEN THAT THING ON YOUR HEAD IS MINE.
HELLO AGAIN, LITTLE MOUSE.
YOU KNOW SOMEONE ELSE WATCHES OVER THESE LANDS.
NO LONGER. SHE IS LONG SINCE DEAD.
CALL OFF YOUR MONGRELS, EREBUS...
OR THEY WILL END UP LIKE THE OTHERS.

OH?
BUT YOU'RE LOOKING A LITTLE OLDER AND THINNER NOW...
MAYBE THE DEAD LEAVES AND WITHERED GRASS HAVE MADE YOU WEAK.
BUT DON'T WORRY, ATLAS...
WE WILL HAVE PLENTY TO FEAST ON SOON...
WE CAN WAIT...
NO...
I'M STARVING!
NO MORE WAITING...
ATLAS!
NO!
NOT YET!
I WANT MOOSE FLESH!

OOOAKKH!
KRACK!!
AAAAAH!
OOOF!
CRASH!

pant
pant
NO! STOP! ALL OF YOU!
THIS IS NOT THE TIME!
I *WARNED* YOU, EREBUS!
GRRRR...
YOU WON'T ALWAYS STAND SO TALL, MOOSE! ALL FEED THE PACK IN THE END!

WE ALL FEED THE WORMS EVENTUALLY, WOLF, EVEN YOU!
WOULD YOU LIKE TO FEED THEM TODAY?!
EH?

OOOOOOOOOOOOOH...
RROOOOO...

pant
pant
OOOH

IT'S BROKEN.

WEAKNESSS

YOU WERE WARNED...
NOW YOU ARE NO USE TO THE PACK.
AROOO?
GROARR!
OOOOOOOOO
THE REST OF MY PACK COMES SOON.
WE'LL SEE YOU AGAIN, ATLAS.

YOU WON'T STAND AGAINST US FOREVER.
RIP
CRUNCH
TEAR
ARE YOU STILL WITH ME, WIX?
I THINK SO.
HANG ON...
WE'RE GETTING OUT OF HERE.

PART VI
THE DELUGE

THE COLONY...
...I'M SORRY...
WE FAILED YOU...
THE ENTIRE PARTY HAS BEEN EATEN?!
WIX...
ORIM'S DAUGHTER IS DEAD, TOO?!
WHAT WILL WE DO NOW?
WE'RE DOOMED!
OH, MASTER ORIM, I'M SO SORRY.
IT ALL HAPPENED SO FAST... I TRIED TO STOP HER.
THIS IS AWFUL!
IN LIGHT OF THIS NEWS, PERHAPS WE SHOULD BEGIN PREPARING TO LEAVE FOR THE CITY.
RESHER!
NOW IS NOT THE TIME!
I'M SORRY, BUT IT MUST BE SAID.
IT HAS CLEARLY BECOME TOO DANGEROUS HERE.
FOUR DAYS...
WHAT?

YOU SAID YOU WOULD GIVE THE SCOUTS FOUR DAYS.
IT HAS ONLY BEEN ONE.
YES, BUT CLEARLY THE MISSION IS A DISASTER...
THEY'RE ALL DEAD.
KESSEL, YOU SAID YOU ACCOUNTED FOR ALL THE BODIES EXCEPT ONE? WIX IS STILL MISSING?
UH...YES... BUT HE WAS CHASED INTO THE FOREST BY TITAN...HE COULDN'T HAVE SURVIVED.
WIX IS AS ABLE AS ANY MOUSE I KNOW, EVEN YOU SCOUTS.
IF YOU DIDN'T SEE THE BODY, WE MUST ASSUME THAT HE IS ALIVE. WE MUST GIVE HIM A CHANCE TO COMPLETE THE MISSION.
BUT, ORIM... CLEARLY YOU ARE DISTRAUGHT...
I IMPLORE THE COUNCIL NOT TO DELAY ANY FURTHER...
FOUR DAYS. HE HAS THREE LEFT...
=cough=
=cough=
THAT IS ALL.

=cough=
NO MORE MEETINGS...
=cough=
=cough=
SIR?
=cough=
=cough=
=gasp!=
MASTER ORIM!
FWUMP
HE'S VERY ILL!
BRING WATER!

WARN ME NEXT TIME YOU WHIP YOUR HEAD AROUND LIKE THAT!
I NEARLY WENT FLYING WITH THAT WOLF!
OH... HEH, SORRY ABOUT THAT.
I FORGOT YOU WERE UP THERE FOR A SECOND.
WILL THEY FOLLOW US?
PROBABLY, BUT NOT TOO CLOSE. THEY'LL KEEP THEIR DISTANCE.
THERE'S EASIER PREY FOR THEM RIGHT NOW.
BACK THERE, YOU SAID SOMEONE WATCHES OVER THE FOREST?
HMM? OH...YES, THE *GUARDIAN*, A GREAT BEAST THAT WATCHES OVER THESE WOODS.
OR DID...
DOES YOUR FOREST HAVE A GUARDIAN?
NOT ANYMORE.

RELEASE!
WHAM!
AWFh!
WOAH!
I JUST TOLD YOU TO WARN ME WHEN YOU--
HUH?
ooph
GOTCHA!

BRACE FOR LANDING!
FWIP!
SPLASH!!
IT'S OK, MOUSE, YOU'RE SAFE NOW.
OUCH... WHAT?
WIX!
WHERE ARE YOU?
ATTACK!!
EEEEEEE!
EH!?

YEEP!
YIP!
YIP!
SNAP!
AGH!
THE WOLF IS GOING DOWN!
WHAT? WOLF?
PRESS THE ATTACK!
AYEEE!
BUMP!
GET OFF ME!!!

WHAT IS ALL THIS RACKET...

HUH?

WHAT IN--

STOP THIS NONSENSE *RIGHT NOW!*

THAT'S NO WOLF, YOU FOOLS!

BUT... IT'S BIG AND IT'S...

BIG.

WOLVES DON'T HAVE ANTLERS!

THAT'S A MOOSE!

BONK!

OW!

MINKA?
YES! YES!

WHAT ARE YOU DOING BACK IN THESE WOODS?
I'M HERE IN SEARCH OF THE GUARDIAN.
THEN I'M HEADING TO SOME PLACE CALLED THE REFUGE.
GUARDIAN? NO ONE'S HEARD FROM HER IN A WHILE.
LIKELY DEAD I SUSPECT--
EXCUSE ME! WHAT'S GOING ON HERE?

LIKE I WAS SAYING ABOUT MICE...
TOUGH LITTLE CRITTERS...
THOUGH THESE SEEM A BIT LOONY.

THIS IS MINKA.
SORRY, CHILD, THEY THOUGHT A WOLF HAD YOU. WE DON'T SEE TOO MANY MOOSE OUT HERE...
AND THEY THINK ANYTHING BIGGER THAN A RABBIT IS A WOLF!
SOME OF US ARE GETTING TIRED OF HIDING IN OUR HOLES AND WANT TO FIGHT BACK. THEY FORGET THAT'S NOT HOW MICE SURVIVE.

NOT THAT THIS FOOL ATTACK WOULD HAVE GONE ANY BETTER AGAINST A REAL WOLF.
SORRY.

WHY AREN'T YOU AT THE REFUGE WITH THE OTHERS?
BAH! WE DON'T NEED NO BEAVERS TO TAKE CARE OF US.
WE CAN MANAGE JUST FINE ON OUR OWN...THOUGH OUR BRIARS HAVE DIED OFF AND OUR HOLES ARE FLOODED.

STILL, WE GET BY.
SAY... YOU LOOK FAMILIAR. HAVE I SEEN YOU BEFORE?
NO, I DON'T THINK SO.
I LIVE IN THE HUMAN HOUSES WITH THE COLONY THERE.
HOUSE MOUSE, EH?
WELL, YOU SURE LOOK FAMILIAR.
THAT FUR...
ANYWAY, YOU'RE WELCOME TO STAY HERE AS LONG AS YOU LIKE. NOT MUCH TO EAT, UNLESS YOU LIKE BARK SOUP.
OOOH... WHAT DID SHE CALL IT?
A MOOSE.
MOOOOOSE.
HEY!
UH, THANKS, BUT WE GOTTA GET MOVING, RIGHT ATLAS?
YEAH, WE HAVE A LONG WAY TO GO.
WELL, BE CAREFUL OUT THERE.
A STORM'S COMING.

YOU'LL FIND THE GUARDIAN'S PLACE JUST OVER THAT HILL.
WATCH YOURSELF OVER THERE. STRANGE CRITTERS AROUND.
THE STREAM IS ON THE OTHER SIDE...
FOLLOW IT UP TO THE BEAVER DAM TO GET TO THE REFUGE.
OK THANKS, MINK.
GOOD TO SEE YOU AGAIN.
SEE?
TOLD YA THERE WERE MICE OUT HERE.
YEAH. I GUESS SO!

JUST OUTSIDE THE COLONY...
"THAT'S THE LAST ONE. NO MORE CATS."
WELL, THAT'S GOOD AT LEAST.
THOSE THINGS LOOK A LOT WORSE, THOUGH.
CRASH
REEOWWWRW!!!
KLANG
ARE THEY GONNA EAT US, UMF?
NAH. DON'T WORRY, MOTTLE, THEY CAN'T GET INSIDE.
WHAT ABOUT THE SCAVENGERS?
THEY'RE GONNA BE DOG FOOD.
THE ELDERS CANCELLED ALL SCAVENGING RUNS FOR NOW.
EVEN MY MISSION TO THE CITY WAS PUT OFF.
SUITS ME.
I'D RATHER STAY HERE.
EXCUSE ME. UMF, ISN'T IT?
UH, YEAH?

MY NAME IS AKAMA. I'M THE AMBASSADOR OF THE SHADE RUN RATS.
I KNOW WHO YOU ARE, MISS AKAMA.
I'VE SEEN YOU AT THE COUNCIL MEETINGS.
I SEE... WELL, ANYWAY, MY RATS AND I ARE BEING RECALLED TO OUR NEST, BUT BEFORE I GO, I WAS HOPING TO SPEAK WITH YOU... PRIVATELY.
YEAH, SURE.
HEY, MOTTLE, BETTER GET INSIDE.
OH. RAT TALK. OK, OK.
WE CAN'T TALK HERE. SORRY FOR THE SECRECY, BUT I NO LONGER TRUST THE MICE.
OH? THEY SEEM OK TO ME.
PERHAPS, BUT SOMETHING STRANGE IS GOING ON.
FOLLOW ME, WILL YOU?
I HAVE SOMETHING TO SHOW YOU.

LATER, ON THE LAKE...
HMM... I DON'T LIKE THIS WEATHER...
I HOPE THE OTHERS HAVE STARTED MAKING THE REPAIRS.
AH, HERE WE ARE...

WELCOME TO **THE DAM.**
WOAH!
YOU **HAVE** BEEN BUSY!
INDEED. THOUGH MOST OF THE DEBRIS WAS PILED UP HERE BEFORE WE ARRIVED.
BUT WE PLUGGED THE HOLES. NOW IT'S A **PROPER** DAM.

THE RAIN IS GETTING WORSE...
ARE YOU SURE YOU WANT TO GO RIGHT NOW?
NO.
BUT I HAVE TO GET BACK AS SOON AS I CAN.
GOOD LUCK TO YOU, MOUSE.
WE'LL SEE YOU SOON.
LONG WAY DOWN...
GUESS I BETTER GET STARTED.
LEAVING WITHOUT SAYING GOODBYE?

OH, HEY, SNAG.
I WASN'T SURE WHERE YOU WERE.
YOU THERE! GET BACK TO **WORK!**
WE HAVE MUCH MORE TO DO!
WE?
YOU JUST STAND THERE BARKING ORDERS! I'LL BE THERE WHEN I'M GOOD AND READY!
hhmph!
SO, HOW DID IT GO WITH THE KING?
OH... OK I GUESS.
TO BE HONEST, HE SEEMS A BIT... *OFF.*
HA HA! YEAH THAT SOUNDS LIKE HIM.
TOLD YA HE WAS A ***FOOL!*** YOU STILL PLAN ON COMING BACK?
MAYBE. WE MIGHT NOT HAVE A CHOICE. BUT RIGHT NOW I HAVE TO WORRY ABOUT GETTING HOME.
STICK TO THE BUSHES, AND YOU'LL BE FINE. THE STREAM WILL LEAD YOU BACK.
STAY TO THIS SIDE OF THE RIVERBED, RODENT! THERE IS WORK GOING ON THE OTHER SIDE AND YOU'LL JUST BE IN THE WAY.
WORK? I THOUGHT THEY WERE FINISHED OVER THERE...
WELL, I BETTER GET GOING.

GOODBYE, SNAG. THANKS AGAIN.
SAFE TRAVELS, MS. MOUSE.
THIS IS HARDER THAN IT LOOKS. SCREW THIS. I'M GOING ACROSS THE STREAM.
HURRY!
WHAT IS TAKING SO LONG?
THE SUPPORT BEAMS ARE DAMAGED...
IT WON'T BE LONG NOW.
WORK QUICKLY!
THE BEAVERS WILL BE ALONG SOON!

ALMOST... GOT IT...
CRACK!
GOT IT!
AWK!
SPLASH
gurgle
KRRRAWK!
KOFF
KOFF
YES! YES!
PISHHH!
WOOOSH!
GROAN
CREEEK!
SNAP!
THE DAM IS WEAKENING!
WE ARE CLOSE NOW!
BROTHERS AND SISTERS, THE FEAST IS NEAR!
I HAVE TO WARN THE BEAVERS!

I TOLD YOU TO KEEP TO THE OTHER SIDE.
THUNK!
SNAG!
I SAW HIM TRAILING YOU.
TOLD YA YOU CAN'T TRUST THESE GRIMY BIRDS.
SQUAWK!
CRAP!
DIDN'T HIT HIM HARD ENOUGH.
I'LL FIX THAT!
CRACK!
CRAWK!

THEY'RE COMING!
RUN!

WHERE DO WE--
SNAG?

GO! I'LL HOLD 'EM OFF!
SNAG!

NO WITNESSES!
MORE!

MEANWHILE...
ARE WE GOING IN?
ENTERING IS FORBIDDEN...
AND UNWISE.
I DON'T THINK HE WOULD FIT, ANYWAY.
WHO'S THAT?
...
WITCHES.
WITCHES?
DO WITCHES EAT MICE?
HMM... WELL...
YOU BETTER STAY UP THERE.

WHAT ARE YOU DOING HERE, MOOSE?
YOU ARE NOT SUPPOSED TO BE HERE YET.
I'M HERE TO SEE THE GUARDIAN.
IS IT DEAD?
NOT DEAD. RESTING.
MOURNING.
HOW DO YOU KNOW?
SISTERS! LOOK AT *THAT!*
IS IT *HIM?*
MY DEAR MOOSE, YOU SEEM TO HAVE PICKED UP A PARASITE.
CAN WE HAVE HIM?
HMM?
NO, HE HAS PLACES TO BE.

INDEED HE *DOES!*
JUST KIDDING, MOOSE.
WE WOULDN'T DARE SEPARATE SUCH A BRAVE KNIGHT FROM HIS LOYAL STEED.
WHAT ARE THEY TALKING ABOUT?
I HAVE NO IDEA.
LADIES, I MUST SPEAK TO THE GUARDIAN.
ALAS, YOU CANNOT.
NO ONE CAN.
SHE WILL NOT STIR UNTIL WINTER ENDS...
AND WINTER WILL NOT END UNTIL SHE STIRS.
MAYBE NOT EVEN THEN.
BUT THIS IS NO NORMAL WINTER...
AND WOLVES HAVE ENTERED THE WOODS.
I'M AFRAID WE DON'T HAVE MUCH TIME.
NONETHELESS...
BETTER GET GOING MOOSE.
THE WEATHER IS WORSENING...
YOU WILL GET WET.
WET? bleh!
WE'RE ALREADY SOAKED...
MAYBE WE SHOULD GO, ATLAS. IT'S GETTING DARK.
HMPH...
I SUPPOSE. MAYBE I'LL GET SOME ANSWERS AT THE DAM...

LATER...

SPLISH

KOFF! ...MORE... WATER... KOFF! KOFF!

KRA-KOOOM!

BROTHERS AND SISTERS! OUR WORK WILL SOON BE REWARDED! THE DARK ONE SENDS THIS RAIN TO WASH AWAY THE BEAVER'S PATHETIC WALL.
OUR MASTER AND HIS MINIONS WILL FEAST FOR A FINAL TIME!
...AND WE WILL BE BLESSED WITH THE SCRAPS!
BUT FIRST...
ONE LAST MEAL FOR OUR PET!
GORGON!
GORGON!
GORGON!
GORGON!
GORGON!
GORGON!
GORGON!
I AM SICK AND TIRED OF BEING DROPPED IN FREEZING WATER BY STUPID BIRDS!
GORGON
GORGON!
LET ME OUT OF HERE!
GORGON!
GORGON!
WHEN THE BEAVERS FIND OUT WHAT YOU DID--
GORGON!
GORGON!
GORGON!
HUH?

THE DAM...
HURRY!
GET THOSE HOLES PLUGGED!
WE HAVE TO REINFORCE THAT SECTION QUICKLY!
ARKEN!
NOT NOW, SQUIRREL!
THE RAVENS!
-huff- -huff-
THEY'VE BEEN UNDERMINING THE DAM!
I KNEW IT!
SO IT WAS THEM!
BUT NO BIRD PECKING COULD DO ALL THIS!
THERE'S BEEN TOO MUCH RAIN!
THAT'S NOT ALL! THEY TOOK THE MOUSE!
-huff-
I TRIED TO STOP THEM.
-huff- -huff-
WE HAVE TO GET HER BACK!
THE MOUSE? PICT!?
WELL... THAT CAN'T BE HELPED NOW!
WE HAVE TO STABILIZE THIS DAM OR THE WHOLE VALLEY WILL--
FSHHH!
PSHHH!
KRAAAACK!

RUN!
KRAKK!
SNAP!

NEARBY...
GORGON!
GORGON!
GORGON!
GORGON!
GORGON!
GORGON!
GORGON!
GORGON!
GORGON!
GORGON!
GORGON!
GORGON!
GORGON!
GORGON!
GORGON!

RUMBLE

SO SOON?
IT BEGINS!

CRASH

DOWNSTREAM...
yawn
ARE WE THERE YET?
NOT MUCH FURTHER I THINK...
RUMBLE
HANG ON!

WIX!
ATLAS!

YOU DON'T STAND SO TALL, NOW, DO YOU?

HE WILL SOON BE EXHAUSTED.
ONCE THE WATER RECEDES...
I WANT HIS SCENT FOUND!

PART VII

STALKER

GET UP, RED MOUSE.
THE CHASE IS NOT OVER.
WHAT'S THE POINT?
I'M JUST A MOUSE.
PATHETIC.

DOWNSTREAM...
FOUND HIM!
IS IT DEAD?
SUCH A PITY.
OH, HE ISN'T DEAD, SISTERS.
HIS CHEST IS STILL MOVING.
cough
cough
gasp!
UHHH... WHA?
HELLO AGAIN.

JUST GET IT OVER WITH QUICKLY.
WE ARE NOT GOING TO EAT YOU, SILLY MOUSE.
WE WOULD NEVER!
OUR BRAVE KNIGHT IS DISCOURAGED. HE HAS LOST HIS NOBLE STEED.
HE DOESN'T LOOK LIKE A KNIGHT TO ME.
HE DOESN'T EVEN HAVE A SWORD.
WE CAN FIX THAT.
CRACK!
THIS WILL DO NICELY.
THERE. NOW, RISE!
UP! UP!

I HEREBY DUB THEE KNIGHT, SIR...
UH...
WHAT WAS YOUR NAME AGAIN?
WIX.
RIGHT. -ahem!-
I HEREBY DUB THEE KNIGHT, SIR WIX!
RISE AND--
-plop-
-sigh- HE WILL NEVER COMPLETE HIS QUEST AT THIS RATE.
OR SLAY THE DRAGON.
OR RESCUE THE DAMSEL.
RESCUE?
HOW CAN I? I'M JUST A MOUSE. I'LL NEVER MAKE IT THAT FAR.
SHE IS PROBABLY ALREADY DEAD.
GO AWAY! LEAVE ME HERE TO DIE IN THE MUD.

BUT YOU'RE SO CLOSE!
IT WOULD BE A SHAME TO GIVE UP NOW!
CLOSE!?
I AM LIFETIMES AWAY.
OH? BUT THE FLOOD WASHED MORE THAN YOU DOWN THAT RIVER.
WHAT?
YOUR FRIEND IS CLOSE, BUT TIME IS RUNNING OUT.
PICT!? CLOSE?
WHERE IS SHE?
HOLD ON THERE! DANGER AWAITS!
AND EVERY GOOD KNIGHT NEEDS A SWORD!

THUNK!
HMM... I GUESS IT'S MORE OF A LANCE THAN A SWORD FOR YOU.
HURRY!
THIS WAY.

NEARBY...

urgh!

WHERE AM I NOW?

I THINK I HEAR THE STREAM UP AHEAD.

SOUNDS LIKE A RIVER NOW.

I MUST BE CLOSER TO HOME.

THERE!
SEE?
PICT!
WAIT!
STAY AWAY!

WELL, THAT DIDN'T GO WELL AT ALL.
TOLD YOU THIS WASN'T GOING TO WORK.
I CAN'T WATCH.
NO, WIX! IT'S A STABBY SWORD! NOT A SLASHY SWORD!
STAB!
STAB!
WIX?
UH...
WACK!

PICT!
AAAGH!

PLOCK!
HISSSSSSSSSSSSSSS
WHERE IS SHE!?

GOT YA!
IT'S COMING!
HURRY!

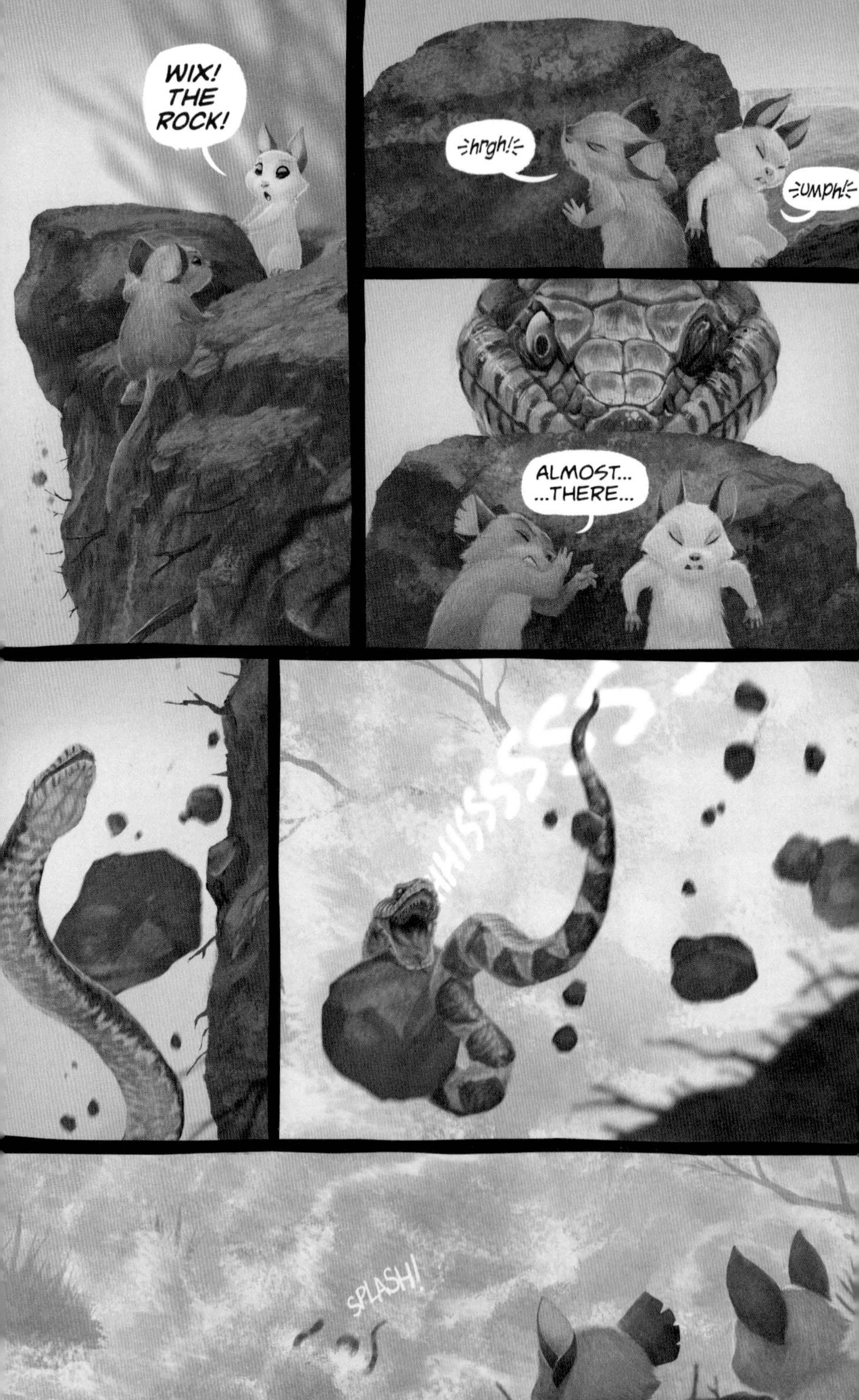
WIX! THE ROCK!
hrgh!
UMPH!
ALMOST...
...THERE...
HISSSSS
SPLASH!

?
?

YOU'RE ALIVE!

OH, WIX!
I NEVER THOUGHT I'D SEE YOU AGAIN!

I KNEW I'D FIND YOU!
BUT HOW DID YOU ESCAPE FROM THE HAWK?
IT'S A LONG STORY.
HUH?

RAVEN!

BEHIND YOU!

WHAT DID YOU DO TO OUR PET?
I GUESS WE'LL HAVE TO FINISH YOU OURSELVES--
CAW?

THERE THEY ARE!
ATTACK!

YOU WILL PAY FOR YOUR TREACHERY, BIRD!

BONK
FLY!
KRAAAH!

WHERE DO WE GO NOW?
FLY TO THE DARK ONE...
WE MUST TELL HIM THE GOOD NEWS!
WE--
!
CRAWK!!!
EXCELLENT CATCH, SISTER!
MMHANK MU
LET'S GO. I THINK OUR LITTLE CHAMPION WILL BE ALRIGHT ON HIS OWN.

IT'S ALRIGHT, WIX. THEY ARE FRIENDS.
HELLO AGAIN, MOUSE. WE WERE SEARCHING FOR SURVIVORS, BUT WE DIDN'T EXPECT TO FIND YOU.
SNAG! YOU'RE OKAY!
OF COURSE I AM! A FEW OLD BIRDS ARE NO MATCH FOR ME.
THE DAM IS...?
DESTROYED. I'M AFRAID THE REFUGE IS NO LONGER A REFUGE.
WILL YOUR KING BE UPSET?
THE KING IS DEAD.
THE LODGE COLLAPSED AND CRUSHED HIM, ALONG WITH HIS AMBITIONS.
ARKEN IS IN CHARGE NOW.
WHAT WILL YOU DO?
WE WILL GO NORTH WITH WHOEVER WANTS TO GO. WE WILL BUILD A NEW DAM UP RIVER. ONE THAT IS NOT SO BIG, I THINK. WE'LL HAVE TO HURRY TO STAY AHEAD OF THE WOLVES.
WILL YOU COME?
NO, I HAVE TO GET HOME.
AARROOOOOOO
I SEE. I--

WOLVES!
BEAVERS! TO THE WATER! WE GO BACK UPSTREAM.
GIVE THESE TWO THE RAFT.
YOU WILL BE SAFER ON WATER.
IF YOUR COLONY IS STILL THERE, THE RIVER WILL TAKE YOU THERE QUICKLY.
BE CAREFUL, MS. MOUSE, AND KEEP AN EYE ON THE SKY. THE WATER WON'T PROTECT YOU FROM BIRDS.
WILL YOU BE ALRIGHT, SNAG?
ME?
OF COURSE! I BET MY OLD TREE ISN'T FLOODED ANYMORE! I'M OFF TO CHECK ON IT NOW.
GOODBYE, MS. MOUSE.
HURRY!
WE MUST GET THE REFUGEES MOVING!
GOOD LUCK TO YOU, MICE.
I DON'T KNOW ABOUT THIS.
WHAT ABOUT THAT SNAKE?
IT PROBABLY WASHED DOWNSTREAM.
erf
IF IT DOES SHOW UP AGAIN, WE'LL STAB HIM WITH THIS.

NEVER STEERED A RAFT BEFORE. I THINK I MIGHT BE GOOD AT THIS...
WIX!
YOU CAME TO LOOK FOR ME!
SURE!
I MEAN... I WAS KINDA CHASED INTO THE WOODS ANYWAY.
FIGURED I MIGHT AS WELL LOOK FOR YOU WHILE I WAS OUT HERE.
NOW WE CAN GO HOME AND PUT ALL THIS BEHIND US.
WAIT-- YOU DON'T KNOW!
IT WAS RESHER! HE SENT THE CATS RIGHT TO YOU!
HE PLANNED THE AMBUSH!
AMBUSH? OF COURSE!
PICT, THERE WAS NO FOOD TRUCK. I WAS AT THE SITE MYSELF.
WHAT? THEN OUR LAST HOPE...
WIX! WE HAVE TO HURRY!
I FEAR SOMETHING TERRIBLE HAS HAPPENED TO THE COLONY.
MY FATHER IS IN DANGER!
I HOPE WE'RE NOT TOO LATE.
DON'T WORRY, PICT.
WE'LL GET BACK IN TIME.

ELSEWHERE...
THE DAM IS DESTROYED!
THE WAY IS CLEAR!

PART VIII

DESTRUCTION MYTHS

THE RIVER...

...YOU SHOULD'VE SEEN HIM, PICT! HE WAS **HUGE!** AND HE HAS THESE...

...UH...

...WHAT WERE THEY CALLED AGAIN... ...**OH YEAH!**

ANTLERS! THEY'RE KINDA LIKE BIG, CRAZY HORNS...

...OH, WAIT --LET ME BACK UP-- DID I MENTION THE GIANT TURTLE? IT WAS EASILY THE BIGGEST ONE I EVER SAW!

IT WASN'T NEARLY AS BIG AS THE MOOSE, BUT STILL, IT WAS PRETTY BIG...

...AT FIRST I THOUGHT IT WAS JUST A BIG ROCK... HEH, IT MIGHT AS WELL HAVE BEEN, BECAUSE IT WAS NO HELP AT ALL!

HE TOLD ME I WAS GONNA **DIE**, AND THEN JUST WANDERED OFF! WHO DOES THAT?

STUPID TURTLE.

OH! AND DID YOU KNOW SOME SQUIRRELS CAN **FLY?** ONE CAME OUT OF NOWHERE AND KNOCKED ME RIGHT OFF ATLAS'S HEAD! THEN--

HEY, PICT, ARE YOU OK?

WHAT IS IT?

YOU WERE RIGHT, WIX. THIS IS NO PLACE FOR A MOUSE. WE WON'T GET ANY HELP OUT HERE.

OH...UM...MAYBE... BUT MICE CAN SURVIVE ALMOST ANYWHERE! I'VE SEEN THEM! RIGHT HERE IN THE FOREST, JUST LIKE YOU SAID!
WELL...THOSE MICE PROBABLY ALL DROWNED IN THE FLOOD...BUT UP UNTIL THEN THEY WERE DOING PRETTY WELL...UM...AND WE'RE DOING OK...

OK?! WE'RE WORSE OFF THAN EVER BEFORE! EVERYTHING OUT HERE IS TRYING TO EAT US!
NOT EVERYTHING...
sigh
MAYBE WE SHOULD JUST GO TO THE CITY LIKE RESHER SAID...
NO!
WE CAN'T DO THAT! I SAW THE CITY FROM THE AIR WHEN THE HAWK HAD ME...
IT...
IT LOOKED BAD.

HMM... WELL, YOUR DAD WILL PROBABLY KNOW WHAT TO DO.
HE ALWAYS DOES.
OH GREAT.
THE RIVER IS ALL CLOGGED UP.
LOOKS LIKE WE'LL HAVE TO GO ON FOOT FROM HERE.
WE HAVE TO HURRY, WIX! THERE ISN'T MUCH TIME!

MEANWHILE...
THE FLOODWATERS RECEDE FROM THE COLONY HOUSE...
KESSEL, RESHER AND HIS MICE TAKE STOCK...
WE FOUND SKEK...
HE FLOATED UP FROM THE BASEMENT.
HE SMELLS WORSE NOW THAN WHEN HE WAS ALIVE.
THE BASEMENT IS COMPLETELY FLOODED!
OUR STASH WAS DOWN THERE!
STASH? YOU WERE HOARDING FOOD DOWN THERE, RESHER?!
WELL, YES... WE WERE STORING A FEW SUPPLIES DOWN THERE...
YOU KNOW THAT IF THINGS GET MUCH WORSE, THE OTHERS WILL RANSACK THE STORE ROOMS.
WE WERE KEEPING THEM SAFE FOR THE JOURNEY TO THE CITY.
SURE YOU WERE. A LOT OF GOOD THAT DID.
WELL, UNFORTUNATELY, THERE ISN'T ENOUGH FOR EVERYONE NOW...
WE'LL HAVE TO LEAVE SOME OF THE WEAKER MICE BEHIND--
EVERYONE GOES, RESHER! THAT WAS THE DEAL.
IF WE NEED MORE FOOD, MY SCOUTS WILL FIND WHAT WE NEED ALONG THE WAY.
OKAY, KESSEL. HAVE IT YOUR WAY...
BUT WE CAN'T WAIT ANY LONGER.
THE ELDERS ARE STILL DITHERING AND THAT DECREPIT OLD ORIM STILL LINGERS ON.
I'M TAKING CARE OF IT.
SO AM I.

ELSEWHERE, IN THE FOREST, THE WOLVES TRUDGE ACROSS THE DRAINED BEAVER LAKE ON THE HUNT FOR MORE PREY...

GRRR...THOSE ON THE ISLAND HAVE PROBABLY ESCAPED NORTH BY NOW!

WE'LL NEVER HUNT THEM DOWN AT THIS RATE!
WE'LL STARVE IN THIS MUD BEFORE WE REACH THEM.
WE SHOULD TURN BACK!
YESSS...

WE GO WHERE I SAY WE GO!

YOU PROMISED US A FEAST!

IF YOU WANT TO EAT, MOVE FASTER!

EREBUS!
HUFF HUFF HUFF
THERE YOU ARE.
WE HAVE RETURNED.
ABOUT TIME! DID YOU FIND HIM?
YES.

WE FOUND THE MOOSE'S SCENT AND TRACKED HIM ACROSS THE RIVER. HE WAS TIRED AND INJURED, BUT HE STILL HAS FIGHT LEFT IN HIM.
THERE WASN'T ENOUGH OF US TO TAKE HIM DOWN.

ALRIGHT, EVERYONE LISTEN TO ME! WE'LL COME BACK FOR THE OTHERS LATER.
IF IT'S MEAT YOU WANT, BRING THAT MOOSE DOWN AND THERE WILL BE ENOUGH FOR US ALL.
FIND THAT MOOSE!

EH?
SNIFF

POACHERS? IN MY WOODS?
WE ARE NOT THE POACHERS HERE, SHADOW WOLF.
YOU ARE.
I CAN'T POACH ON MY OWN LANDS.
THESE ARE NOT YOUR LANDS, AND YOU WON'T BE HERE MUCH LONGER.
WE HAVE SEEN IT. YOUR END COMES SOON.
SHE COMES SOON.
WHO? YOUR GUARDIAN?
HA!
I'M NOT AFRAID OF GHOSTS, OR THE SILLY STORIES YOU TELL.
YOU SHOULD BE AFRAID.
AND SHE ISN'T ALL YOU SHOULD BE AFRAID OF...
ENOUGH. I'LL FIND YOU EVENTUALLY.
UNTIL THEN...
I HAVE HUNTING TO DO.

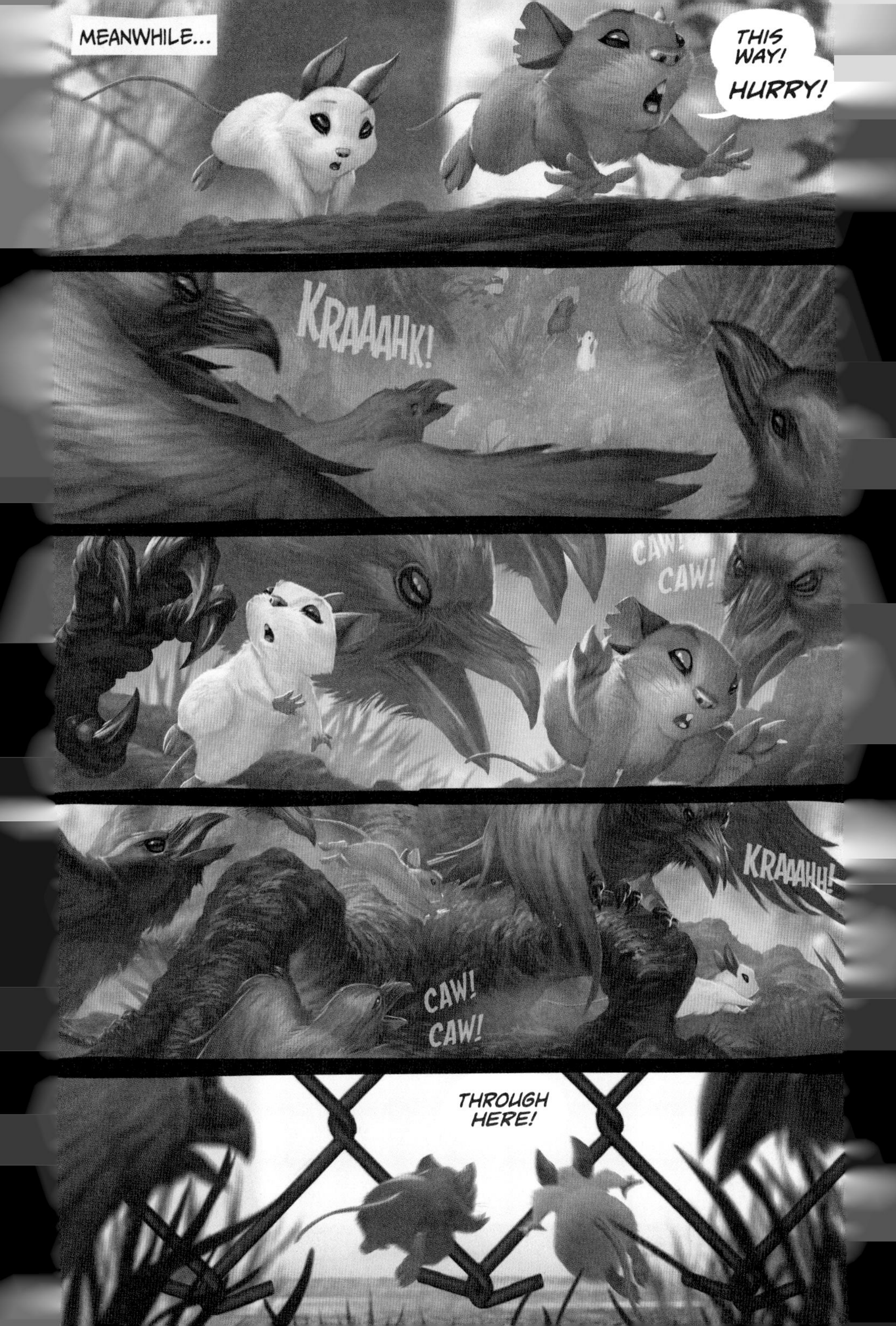
MEANWHILE...
THIS WAY! HURRY!
KRAAAHK!
CAW! CAW!
KRAAAHH!
CAW! CAW!
THROUGH HERE!

ooph
SPLASH!
ARE YOU OK?
YEAH...
COME ON!
STRANGE...
KRAAAHH!
CAW!
CAW!
THEY AREN'T FOLLOWING...
LOOK!
OWL!

DO YOU THINK IT SEES US?
IF WE CAN SEE IT, IT CAN SEE US.
GET READY. WE'LL SPLIT UP.
IT CAN'T GET US BOTH.
DON'T WORRY ABOUT THAT OLD THING, LITTLE MICE.
IT'S MADE OF WOOD, YOU SEE?
HUMANS PUT IT UP THERE TO SCARE THE PIGEONS AND CROWS AWAY...
...AND MICE, TOO, I SUPPOSE.
BUT YOU'RE NOT AFRAID NOW...
ARE YOU?

HELLO THERE. YOU'VE COME FROM THE WOODS, YES?
I DIDN'T THINK THERE WERE ANY OF YOU LEFT.

OH! IT'S THE HAWKRIDER...
HUH?

"I SAW YOU AS YOU FLEW OVER."

YOU DID? YOU MUST HAVE GOOD EYESIGHT.
YES, YES. YOU BOTH MUST BE VERY TIRED.
FOLLOW ME. THE OTHERS ARE HERE AS WELL.

OTHERS?

THAT'S A BIG RAT.
OH. ARE THEY DANGEROUS?
THAT'S A POSSUM -OR OPOSSUM- I DON'T KNOW WHICH THEY PREFER.
GUESS WE'RE ABOUT TO FIND OUT.

COME. COME.
THIS WAY.
THE FLOODING PILED UP ALL THIS GARBAGE, YOU SEE.
STOP
THE WATER PUSHED THE GREAT WHEELED BEAST EVER SO SLIGHTLY AWAY FROM THE ENTRANCE.
JUST ENOUGH...
UP HERE.
IT CAN'T BE...

THERE IS SO MUCH FOOD!
HOW IS THIS POSSIBLE?
I DON'T KNOW...I GUESS THE HUMANS MISSED IT.

LOOK! SOMEONE ELSE IS HERE!
skritch
scratch
skritch

pop

HEY! IT'S THE MOOSE MOUSE! AND A FRIEND!
HELLO AGAIN.

OH, IT'S YOU! WELCOME!

MINKA? YOU'RE ALIVE!
YEP! STILL KICKING. I THOUGHT THE FLOOD WAS GONNA DROWN US ALL, BUT MOST OF US WASHED UP HERE.
I GUESS THAT DAM FINALLY BROKE, HUH? STUPID BEAVERS!
THERE'S SO MUCH FOOD!
YEAH. PLENTY TO GO AROUND. I SUSPECT MORE SURVIVORS WILL SHOW UP SOON, BUT THERE SHOULD BE ENOUGH TO LAST FOR AWHILE.
WIX! THERE MUST BE MONTHS OF FOOD! WE CAN BRING THE OTHERS HERE!
I GUESS SO. BUT WHAT HAPPENS WHEN WE RUN OUT AGAIN?
THERE SHOULD BE ENOUGH TO GET US THROUGH THESE STRANGE TIMES.
NOT LIKELY.
THE WEATHER WON'T CHANGE UNTIL THE SHADOW IS GONE AND THE GUARDIAN COMES.
BAH! PAY NO MIND TO THAT CRAZY OLD POSSUM.
YOU TWO MUST BE EXHAUSTED. WE HAVE SOME PLACES IN THE BACK WHERE YOU CAN REST.
AND GRAB WHATEVER FOOD YOU LIKE.
THANKS, BUT WE MUST GET BACK HOME!
MINKA'S RIGHT, WE SHOULD REST A BIT FIRST. WE HAVE A LONG WAY TO GO.
BUT...YES. I SUPPOSE YOU'RE RIGHT. A COUPLE OF HOURS WILL HELP.
THIS WAY.

LATER...
SOMEWHERE.
LYING
DOWN
AGAIN?

ARE YOU
REALLY DONE
RUNNING?

HOW
BORING.
WE HAVE
EVERYTHING
WE NEED. I
CAN STOP
NOW.
YOU KNOW
IT WON'T
LAST. MORE
WILL COME.

THERE ARE
ALWAYS MORE
MICE TO FEED.
TOO
MANY.

YOU
BREED
LIKE...
MICE.
WHAT
WILL YOU DO
WHEN YOU RUN
OUT OF FOOD
AGAIN?

ONLY
THE DEAD
CAN REST
NOW.

KEEP
MOVING...
OR
DIE.

ANOTHER DREAM.

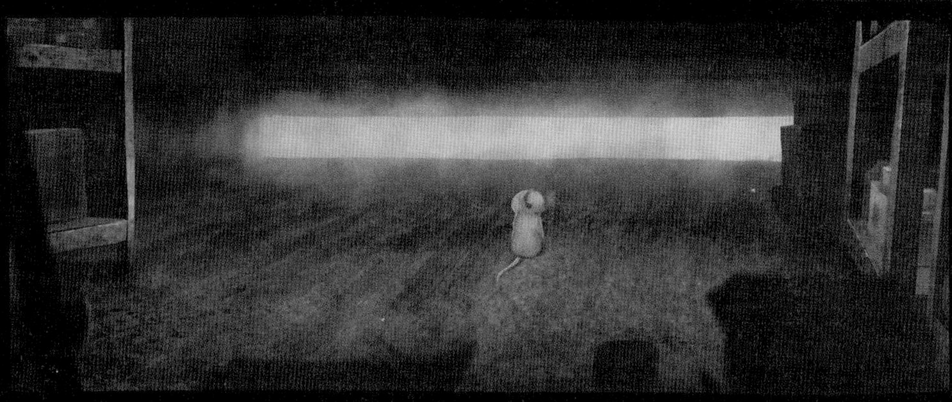

CAN'T SLEEP, LITTLE MOUSE?
SOMETHING ON YOUR MIND?

POSSUM, WHAT WAS ALL THAT TALK ABOUT SHADOWS AND GUARDIANS?

THE TREES WHISPER THE FUTURE TO THOSE WHO CAN HEAR THEM.
CAN YOU HEAR THEM?
NO. BUT YOU KNOW WHO CAN. YOU'VE MET THEM.
THE WITCHES?
YES. I SPEAK TO THEM, TOO, SOMETIMES.
THEY SAID SOMETHING ABOUT A GUARDIAN...
THE GUARDIAN, YES!
THEY SAY SHE'S IN HER CAVE AND WON'T COME OUT.
THEY SAY A CURSE HAS BEEN PLACED ON HER.
CURSE? THERE IS A CURSE NOW?
I DON'T UNDERSTAND ANY OF THIS.
I MAY NOT KNOW THE FUTURE, BUT I KNOW HOW THINGS CAME TO BE THIS WAY...
IN A MANNER...
PERHAPS THAT WILL HELP.
ONCE, THE FOREST HAD A GREAT GUARDIAN TO WATCH OVER IT...

"EMPRESS!
"NO ONE CHALLENGED HER IN THE FOREST.
"FOR YEARS, SHE PROTECTED THE FOREST AND KEPT THE WOLVES AWAY.
"SHE WAS CUNNING, TOO. MOST HUMANS NEVER KNEW SHE WAS THERE, AND THE FEW WHO DID STAYED AWAY.
"THIS EMPRESS HAD AN HEIR...
"A LITTLE PRINCE, YOU SEE.
"HE WAS MUCH LOVED BY EVERYONE IN THE FOREST.
SPLASH
"THE ANIMALS WERE SAFE IN THE FOREST FROM OUTSIDERS.
"BUT FAR AWAY IN THE CITY, SOMETHING WAS HAPPENING...

"I DON'T KNOW WHAT IT WAS, BUT IT DROVE THE HUMANS MAD.
POLICE
POLICE
"I WATCHED AS THEY FOUGHT EACH OTHER IN THE STREETS.
"THEIR INSANITY SPREAD,
BREAKING NEWS
"...UNTIL EVENTUALLY THEY WERE AT WAR ALL OVER THE WORLD!
"FINALLY, IN THEIR MADNESS, THEY EVEN WARRED AGAINST THE STARS THEMSELVES!
"THEY SENT THEIR MOST POWERFUL WEAPON TO DESTROY THEM.
"BUT THE STARS HAD WEAPONS OF THEIR OWN..."
WEAPONS? WHAT KIND OF WEAPONS?
HMM... HOW CAN I EXPLAIN... OH...

"...**WOLVES!**
GREAT WOLVES! THREE OF THEM CAME, EACH WITH THEIR WOLFPACKS. I SAW THEM!"

"WOLVES?"

"OF A SORT... FIRST CAME THE ***FIRE WOLF***, MOST POWERFUL AND TERRIBLE, AND MOTHER TO ALL THE OTHERS. HER BURNING FANGS BIT DEEP INTO THE CITY."

"FIRE WOLF?"

"YES!"

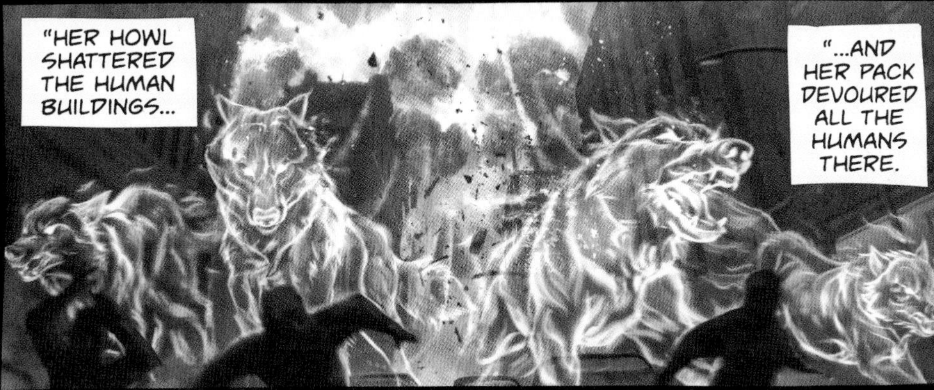

"HER HOWL SHATTERED THE HUMAN BUILDINGS...

"...AND HER PACK DEVOURED ALL THE HUMANS THERE.

"I SAW HER, AS DID MANY OTHERS...

"SOME WERE BLINDED, AND OTHERS WERE DRIVEN MAD AT THE SIGHT OF HER.

"MOST DISMISSED IT AS A HUMAN AFFAIR, BUT EMPRESS WAS WORRIED.

"SHE WAS RIGHT TO BE, FOR THAT WAS ONLY THE BEGINNING.
"THE SECOND WOLF CAME NEXT, THE SKY WOLF, AND SWALLOWED THE SUN.
"HIS PACK SWIRLED THROUGH THE WOODS, KILLING PLANT AND ANIMAL ALIKE WITH THEIR POISONOUS BREATH.
"MANY IN THE FOREST DIED THEN, BUT NO DEATH WAS FELT AS MUCH AS THAT OF THE LITTLE PRINCE.
"EMPRESS WAS OVERCOME WITH GRIEF...
"SHE RETREATED TO HER CAVE.
"NO ONE HAS SEEN HER SINCE.
"MOST BELIEVE SHE IS DEAD, BUT THE WITCHES SAY OTHERWISE."

IN ANY CASE, IT BECAME TERRIBLY COLD AFTER THAT, DO YOU REMEMBER?
YES.
THAT'S BECAUSE OUR GUARDIAN EMPRESS LEFT US, YOU SEE? SHE DID MORE THAN PROTECT THE FOREST. SHE KEPT IT ***ALIVE!***

"NOW, THE THIRD GREAT WOLF, ***EREBUS,*** AND HIS PACK, COME TO SCOUR THE WORLD OF WHAT REMAINS...

"HE IS THE SHADOW OF HIS BROTHER IN THE SKY, AND HE WILL FEAST ON THIS DYING WORLD UNTIL THERE IS NOTHING LEFT."

CAN NO ONE STOP HIM? WHAT ABOUT THE GUARDIAN?
THE CURSE, REMEMBER?
THE WITCHES SAY THE SHADOW WOLF PUT A SPELL ON HER. SHE WILL NOT LEAVE HER CAVE UNTIL HE IS DEAD, AND THE WEATHER WILL NOT CHANGE WHILE SHE SLEEPS AND HE RULES.

BUT WHO ELSE CAN KILL A WOLF?
ONE CAN...
ATLAS!
WELL...

HEY! THERE YOU ARE.
YOU SHOULD HAVE WOKE ME UP! WE BETTER GET GOING.
HELLO AGAIN.
OH HEY, PICT. YEAH, I GUESS WE SHOULD GO.
THANKS FOR THE STORY, POSSUM.
WE HAVE TO GET HOME NOW.
SAFE TRAVELS, LITTLE MICE.
WHAT WAS THAT ABOUT?
UMM... I'M NOT SURE.

PART IX

HOMECOMING

WE'RE ALMOST THERE!
SLOW DOWN!
gasp LOOK!
A MOUSE!
HE'S DEAD!
IT MUST BE ONE OF THE WILD MICE THAT DROWNED.
NO...I KNOW THIS MOUSE.
HE IS ONE OF THE SCOUTS WE SENT TO THE CITY WEEKS AGO.
HE'S BEEN HERE A WHILE. NONE OF THE SCAVENGERS HAVE EATEN HIM...
DON'T TOUCH HIM!
WHAT ARE ALL THOSE SORES?
HE LOOKS... BURNED.
FIRE WOLVES...
HUH?
NOTHING.

THIS MUST HAVE HAPPENED IN THE CITY! HE MUST HAVE GOTTEN LOST ON THE WAY BACK AND DIED HERE.
WIX! WE HAVE TO HURRY!
WE HAVE TO STOP RESHER!
IF HE CONVINCES THE COLONY TO GO TO THE CITY, THEY COULD ALL END UP THE SAME!
WAIT!
NOT OUT IN THE OPEN.
LOOK!
THE HAWK IS BACK!
THIS WAY.
STAY LOW.

LATER...
WE'RE CLOSE...
THE HOUSE! WE'RE ALMOST HOME!
WHAT'S THAT NOISE?
RUSTLE
RUSTLE
RUSTLE
SOMETHING'S COMING!
WIX!
I KNEW YOU WERE ALIVE! AND PICT, TOO!
OOF

UMF!
GOOD TO SEE YOU, TOO, YA BIG RAT.
WHAT ARE YOU DOING OUT HERE?
LOOKING FOR YOU!
AKAMA SHOWED ME THE PLACE WHERE THE CATS ATTACKED!
I SAW THAT OUR USUAL ESCAPE ROUTES WERE BLOCKED OFF... VERY STRANGE.
WE CAME TO THE WOODS TO LOOK FOR SURVIVORS AND FOUND TITAN'S BODY, BUT THERE WAS NO SIGN THAT YOU HAD BEEN EATEN, SO I STAYED OUT HERE TO LOOK FOR YOU.
I KNEW THE CATS DIDN'T GET YOU GUYS!
BUT THEN THIS HUGE WALL OF WATER CAME AND NEARLY WASHED ME AWAY! I HAD TO HANG ON TO A TREE FOR DEAR LIFE! I THOUGHT I WAS--
UMF... WHERE IS AKAMA NOW? IS SHE...?
OH, SHE'S FINE! HER RATS RECALLED HER TO THEIR NEST, SO SHE WENT HOME.
OH! IT'S TOO BAD THAT SHE'S GONE. SHE WAS ONE OF THE FEW WE COULD TRUST IN THE COUNCIL...
HOW ARE THINGS IN THE COLONY, UMF?
IS RESHER STILL MAKING TROUBLE?
OH IT'S...
...UH...
I HAVE TO TELL YOU...
...YOUR FATHER...
WHAT IS IT?
PICT, HE'S VERY SICK. HE COLLAPSED IN THE LAST MEETING...
COLLAPSED!?
YES. THEY TOOK HIM TO HIS ROOM-
WE HAVE TO GO!
COME ON!

INSIDE, TWO GUARDS STAND VIGIL AT THE ENTRANCE OF ORIM'S ROOM...

P-PICT?
IS THAT REALLY YOU?

YES. IS MY FATHER ALRIGHT?
I HAVE TO SEE HIM.

UH, WE HAVE ORDERS NOT TO LET ANYONE IN-
ARE YOU GONNA STOP ME?!

DAD!

OH NO...

HE'S VERY DEHYDRATED...
HE NEEDS WATER.

DRINK.
NO...
NO WATER...

SNIFF
SNIFF

NO!
WIX!
SLAP!

WHAT IS IT?
POISON!

ARE YOU SURE?
WIX IS NEVER WRONG ABOUT POISON.

YES...
...POISON...
...EH?

PICT? AM I HALLUCINATING? IS IT YOU?
YES! YES FATHER! IT'S ME!

DAUGHTER! IT IS YOU! YOU'RE ALIVE!
cough
cough
REST NOW.

WIX! YOU'RE HERE, TOO! WONDERFUL!
THE MISSION... DID YOU FIND FOOD?
WE FOUND ENOUGH FOR THE WHOLE COLONY. IT WILL LAST US A LONG TIME.

GOOD. GOOD. THEN THE COLONY IS SAVED.
PICT, YOU MUST STOP RESHER. HE IS TRYING TO TAKE OVER. YOU MUST LEAD THE COLONY NOW.

I'LL STOP HIM, FATHER. AND YOU'LL LEAD US AGAIN IN NO TIME.

I HAVE BEEN POISONED FOR SOME TIME NOW... SMALL AMOUNTS... I DIDN'T REALIZE...
...IT'S TOO LATE NOW.

DON'T SAY THAT. YOU'LL BE FINE.
LISTEN TO ME. YOU ARE READY. I SEE THAT NOW.
THE OTHERS...THEY ARE AFRAID... YOU MUST CONVINCE THEM TO LISTEN TO YOU.
I WILL.

WHERE DID THOSE GUARDS GO?
HEY, LET'S GIVE THEM SOME TIME ALONE. LET'S GO FIND SOME CLEAN WATER.
THERE IS NO NEED FOR THAT...
HE'S GONE.

WHERE ARE YOU GOING?
TO TAKE CARE OF RESHER.

NEARBY...
RESHER!
OH, CAPTAIN KESSEL, YOU'RE HERE, TOO!
WHY AREN'T YOU AT YOUR POST?
IT'S PICT! SHE'S ALIVE!
WHAT? HOW IS THAT POSSIBLE?
THIS CAN'T BE...
SHE'S IN ORIM'S ROOM NOW. THAT RED MOUSE FROM THE EXPEDITION IS WITH HER, TOO!
INCREDIBLE!
KESSEL, SHE KNOWS ABOUT US!
SHE KNOWS ABOUT YOU.
DON'T EVEN TRY SELLING ME OUT! YOU ARE PART OF THIS, TOO!
IF SHE TELLS THE OTHERS...
WE HAVE TO DEAL WITH HER AND WE DON'T HAVE MUCH TIME. IF THEY ARE STILL IN HER FATHER'S ROOM, WE CAN KILL THEM ALL.
NO.
THAT'S TOO FAR. THIS HAS ALL GONE TOO FAR.
KESSEL! I'M WARNING YOU--
YOU DON'T WARN ME, RESHER!
THIS IS OVER! I SHOULD HAVE NEVER LISTENED TO YOU IN THE FIRST PLACE!

I DON'T THINK YOU UNDERSTAND WHAT IS GOING ON HERE! DO YOU REALLY THINK YOU ARE IN CHARGE, CAPTAIN?
OF COURSE I AM! WITHOUT MY SCOUTS, YOU WOULDN'T LAST A DAY OUT THERE!
WHAT? WHAT ARE YOU TALKING ABOUT?
YOUR SCOUTS? KESSEL, YOU HAVEN'T BEEN PAYING ATTENTION.
ENOUGH! YOU HAVE OUTLIVED YOUR USEFULNESS, KESSEL.
OUTLIVED MY...
YOU'VE GONE MAD, RESHER!
GUARDS, ARREST HIM!
DID YOU HEAR ME? I SAID TO AR--
HUH?

UGHHRK!
SHIKT

GOODBYE, KESSEL.
WHAT DID YOU DO?!
WHAT WAS NECESSARY.
NO MORE WAITING, BOYS. WE'RE TAKING OVER.
IT'S TIME FOR US TO GO.
GET THE OTHERS WHO ARE LOYAL TO US AND CLEAR OUT AS MUCH AS YOU CAN FROM THE STORE ROOM.
WE'LL NEED A DISTRACTION.
YOU'LL HAVE IT.
HAND THAT TO ME.
YOU TWO GET TO THE UTILITY ROOM. IT'S TIME.
YOU KNOW WHAT TO DO.
WHAT ABOUT ORIM AND HIS DAUGHTER? AND THE RED MOUSE?
DOES THE COLONY KNOW THEY ARE BACK?
I DON'T THINK SO.
GOOD. I'LL DEAL WITH THEM MYSELF.

MAIN ROOM...

gasp!
IS THAT WHO I THINK IT IS?

PICT!
IT'S REALLY HER!

LOOK!
NO!

SHE IS ALREADY OUT!
WHAT NOW?
WE STALL.

PICT! HOW WONDERFUL TO SEE YOU!
MURDERER!

I KNOW IT WAS YOU WHO KILLED MY *FATHER!*

WHAT?
MASTER ORIM IS DEAD?
WHAT? ORIM IS DEAD?
AND YOU THINK I...
PICT, YOU'VE BEEN THROUGH SO MUCH. THE TRAUMA YOU'VE EXPERIENCED... LET'S TALK ABOUT THIS IN PRIVATE.
NO!
EVERYONE SHOULD HEAR THIS!
WE KNOW YOU WERE BEHIND THE AMBUSH OF OUR PARTY BY THE CATS!
ME!? IS THAT SUPPOSED TO BE A JOKE? HOW ON EARTH COULD I CONTROL THOSE BEASTS?
YOU TOLD THEM WHERE THE MICE WOULD BE, AND YOUR LACKEYS SEALED OFF THE EXITS.
THIS IS RIDICULOUS! AND HOW IS IT THAT THIS MOUSE SURVIVED WHEN ALL THE OTHER, MORE EXPERIENCED MICE WERE KILLED? MAYBE HE WAS THE ONE BEHIND THIS.
YOU WERE LEADING THEM AT THE TIME, CORRECT?
YOU WON'T TALK YOUR WAY OUT OF THIS!
FRIENDS! I HEARD HIM TALKING ABOUT THE AMBUSH.
THEY USED CATNIP TO LURE THE CATS!

HUH?

"THOSE ARE THE MICE THAT WERE GUARDING ORIM'S ROOM...
"THEY WALKED OUT WITH RESHER JUST NOW...

"WHERE ARE THEY SLINKING OFF TO?"

UMF, KEEP AN EYE ON PICT. I'LL BE RIGHT BACK.

HUH? WHERE ARE YOU GOING?
I'LL BE RIGHT BACK!

RESHER WOULD HAVE KILLED ME, TOO, IF I HADN'T ESCAPED!
HE AND HIS CRONIES CHASED ME OUT OF THE HOUSE!

IS THIS TRUE, RESHER?

OF COURSE NOT, ELDERS! THIS IS *INSANE!*

YOU THERE! YOU'RE A GUARD! GO GET CAPTAIN KESSEL! HE NEEDS TO HEAR THIS.
THEN HE WILL ARREST YOU, RESHER!
=hhmph= YES, LET'S WAIT FOR KESSEL. WE NEED A VOICE OF REASON.
DOWN THE HALL...
WHERE DID THEY GO?
PUSH!
I AM PUSHING!

THIS IS CRAZY! I CAN'T BELIEVE IT'S COME TO THIS.

MAYBE RESHER HAS LOST IT...
HURRY UP AND FIND THE MATCHES! WE HAVEN'T GOT ALL DAY!
WHAM!

I'LL EMPTY OUT THE LIGHTER FLUID.
BOUNCE!
BOUNCE!
squirt!
squirt!

LIGHTER FLUID? MATCHES?
ARE THEY STARTING A FIRE?

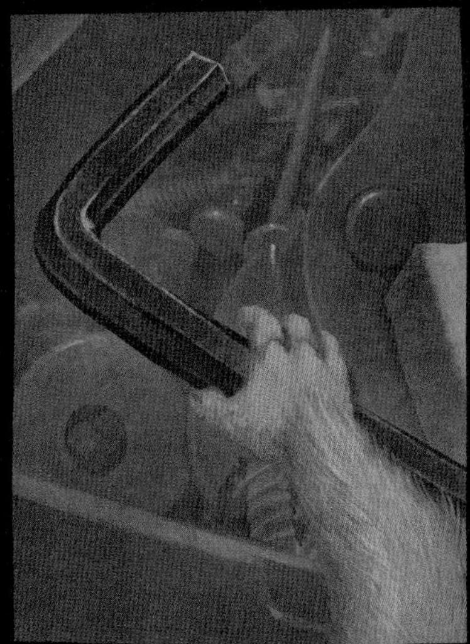

I HAVE TO STOP THEM.

FOUND 'EM!
HUH?
BEHIND YOU!
KLANK
FWIP!
SWIPE!
ooph!

SNAP!

WOOOSH!

MEANWHILE...
WHAT ARE THEY UP TO OVER THERE?
I DON'T LIKE THIS...
WHERE IS KESSEL?
DOES ANYONE KNOW WHERE HE IS?
RESHER, OUR MICE ARE IN THE STOREROOM. THEY'RE WAITING ON YOUR SIGNAL.
TELL THEM TO BEGIN. THERE WON'T BE ANY RESISTANCE SOON.
ENOUGH OF THIS! EVERYONE, LISTEN TO ME! THE TIME HAS COME! WE CAN'T STAY HERE ANY LONGER!
WE MUST TAKE ACTION! MY MICE ARE GATHERING THE FOOD AND SUPPLIES NOW...
WHAT? WHO AUTHORIZED THIS?
I DID.
WE ARE LEAVING FOR THE CITY AT ONCE.
NO! WE CAN'T!
RESHER, I'VE SEEN THE CITY! WE CAN'T GO THERE! IT IS IN RUINS!
RUINS?
WHAT WILL WE DO? WHERE WILL WE GO?
LIES!
SHE IS TRYING TO FRIGHTEN US.
IT'S TRUE, RESHER! BUT WE'VE FOUND ANOTHER PLACE NOT FAR FROM HERE WITH EVERYTHING WE NEED!
OH? WELL, THAT'S WONDERFUL!
RESHER, WE WILL NOT FOLLOW YOU. AND WE WILL NOT ALLOW YOU TO TAKE THE SUPPLIES.
THE CHOICE IS NO LONGER YOURS, ELDER.
YOU AREN'T IN CHARGE HERE, RESHER!
YEAH!
WE'RE WITH PICT!
EH? FINE. STAY AND STARVE, BUT WE ARE TAKING WHAT WE NEED!

I'VE SEEN WHAT HAPPENED TO THE SCOUTS WE SENT TO THE CITY! ANYONE WHO GETS CLOSE WILL DIE!
IF YOU WANT TO DIE OUT THERE, BE MY GUEST. BUT YOU AREN'T TAKING ANYTHING WITH YOU!

I'VE HAD ENOUGH OF THIS!

HUH?!

GET BACK, YOU DISGUSTING RAT!

KESSEL!
huff
huff

WE FOUND KESSEL!
HE'S BEEN STABBED!
HE'S DEAD!

WHAT?! NO!
RESHER!
YOU DID THIS!

LOOKS LIKE THERE'S GONNA BE A FIGHT.
YEP.
HEY, DO YOU GUYS SMELL...

FIRE!

RUN!

WE HAVE TO GET TO THE STOREROOM!
NO TIME FOR THAT!

WARN THE OTHERS! HELP THEM MOVE THE PUPS AND INJURED.
Y-YES. ALRIGHT.

RUN!
WE GOTTA GET OUT OF HERE!
EVERYONE! MEET UP IN THE BACKYARD! STAY TOGETHER! THERE IS TIME, BUT WE MUST HURRY!
WIX...
UMF, WHERE DID WIX RUN OFF TO THIS TIME?
UMM... HE WENT THAT WAY.
NO!
COME ON!

NEARBY...
NO WITNESSES.
STAY BACK!
HUH?
SCRRRAPE!
AAAAAAAH!!!

OOF
ACK!!!

HUH?
WOOOSH!
AGHHH!!!
AAARGH!!!

WIX!
WHERE ARE YOU!

I CAN'T SEE ANYTHING!
COUGH! COUGH! COUGH!
I'LL KEEP LOOKING. GET OUT OF HERE!

NO! WIX TOLD ME TO KEEP AN EYE ON YOU-
HELP!

I'M STUCK!

MOTTLE!

ERGGH!!!
HURRY!

MOTTLE!

COME ON! QUICKLY NOW!

HRRRGGH!!!

PICT...

PICT!

I...I'M OK!

THE WAY IS BLOCKED! TAKE MOTTLE AND GET OUT OF HERE.

I'LL FIND ANOTHER WAY OUT!

HELLO, PICT.

I DIDN'T WANT TO LEAVE WITHOUT SAYING GOODBYE.

I'VE BEEN LOOKING FORWARD TO THIS FOR A LONG TIME!

KRACK!
AAAGH!!!

NO WAY OUT DOWN HERE!
COME BACK HERE!

MAYBE UPSTAIRS...

GOTTA GET TO THE ROOF...
ONLY WAY OUT...

WAIT...

WAS THAT...
OH GREAT!
MORE TROUBLE!

NO TURNING BACK NOW...

YOU... OOMF YOU CAN'T RUN FOREVER!

ELSEWHERE...
cough!
cough!
cough!
cough!
hack!
GOTTA FIND A WAY OUT...
cough!
cough!
cough!
CAN'T...
...BREATHE...
PATHETIC RED MOUSE.
gasp!
LYING DOWN AGAIN?
THATS A SHAME...
...I WAS HOPING FOR A GOOD CHASE!

GOTTA... GET UP!

YESSSS!!!

HA HA HAHAHA!

THE STAIRS!

DEAD END!

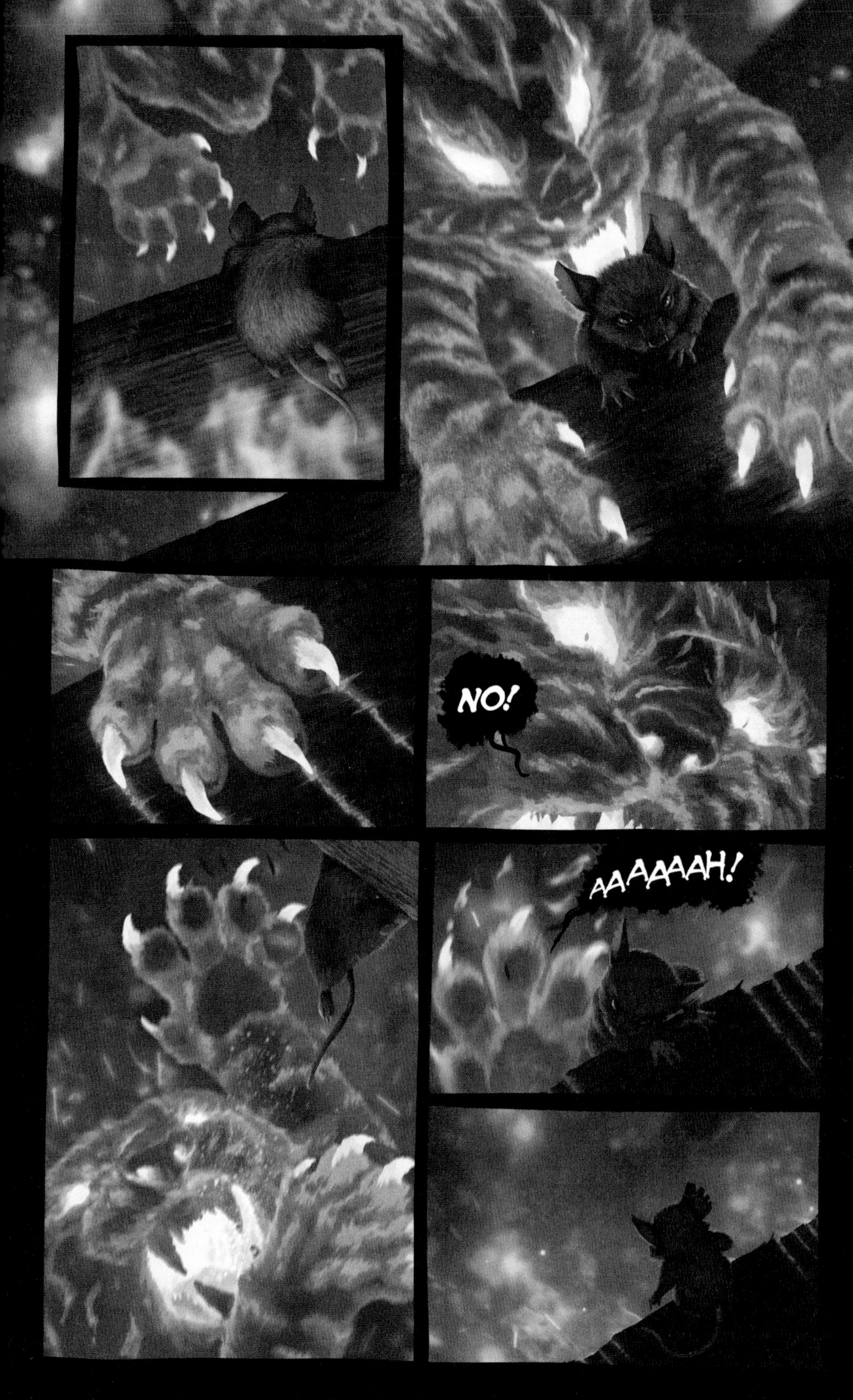
NO!
AAAAAAH!

OUTSIDE...
koff!
koff!
gasp!
koff! koff!
koff!
HA! HA! THERE YOU ARE!
WHERE ARE YOU GOING?
PICT...
IT'S OVER, PICT...
THERE IS NOWHERE LEFT TO FLEE!

FLEE?
I'M NOT FLEEING FROM YOU, RESHER...
...I'M LURING YOU.
?
NO...

NOOOOOOOOOOOOOOOOOOOOOOOOOO!

GOODBYE, RESHER.

THIS WHOLE PLACE IS ABOUT TO COME DOWN...
OOF!

WIX?
KOFF! KOFF! KOFF!

WIX!
YOU MADE IT!
=hrrrgh!=
WHA--?
BEHIND YOU!
WOAH!
AGHH!

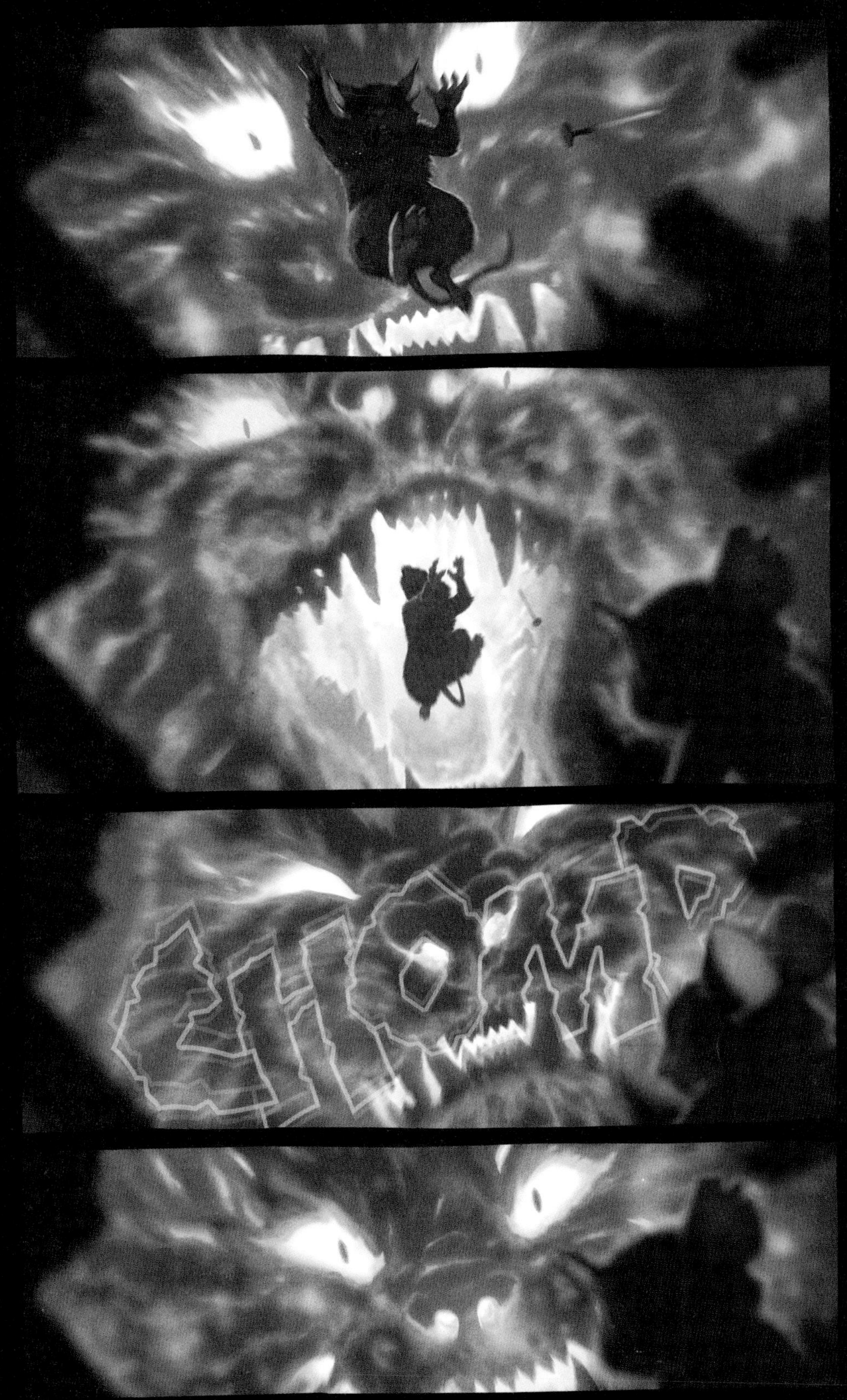
CHOMP

WE GOTTA GET OFF THIS ROOF!
THIS WAY!

DOES ANYONE SEE THEM?

THERE!

LOOK!

YOU MADE IT!
OF COURSE WE DID!

SO WHAT DO WE DO NOW?

PART X

CURSE BREAKER

THE NEXT MORNING...
I'M SO TIRED.
NOT FAR NOW! JUST THIS WAY.
THE OWL!
WE'RE HERE!
THE DOOR...
OH NO...

WHAT A MESS!

LOOK!
A WOLF!

MOOSE MOUSE! AND EVEN MORE FRIENDS!

YOU MISSED IT!

IT WAS TERRIBLE!
WOLVES! AND YOUR MOOSE.
WHAT HAPPENED!?
ATLAS!?

"HE WAS BEING CHASED BY THE WOLVES!
"HE RAN IN THE STORE TO GET AWAY, BUT THEY FOLLOWED HIM.

"THEY FOUGHT AND FOUGHT UNTIL HE BASHED HIS WAY INTO THE BACK ROOM.
"HE DIDN'T KNOW WE WERE HERE.

"HE GOT ONE OF THEM...

"THE REST OF THE WOLVES WERE DISTRACTED WITH ALL THE FOOD AND MICE RUNNING AROUND.
"THEY RANSACKED THE PLACE...
"...AND GOT A FEW MICE, TOO.

"THE RAVENS CAME WITH THEM AND CARRIED OFF A LOT OF STUFF.
"THEY TOOK OFF WITH MY NUTS!"

ATLAS! WHERE DID HE GO?
HE ESCAPED THROUGH THE BACK. HE WAS BADLY HURT, I DON'T KNOW HOW FAR HE GOT.
I'M AFRAID THE WOLVES WENT AFTER HIM NOT LONG AFTER.
PICT, THE FOOD...YOU SAID THERE WOULD BE FOOD?
OH... WELCOME, FRIENDS! YOU MUST BE HUNGRY.
DON'T WORRY, THEY DIDN'T GET IT ALL. THERE IS STILL SOME FOR YOU.
THERE WON'T BE ENOUGH NOW...
MORE ANIMALS WILL COME...
MORE ANIMALS COME EVERY DAY. THE DOOR IS BROKEN OPEN NOW.
WE CAN'T LEAVE WHAT'S LEFT OUT IN THE OPEN LIKE THIS. WE NEED TO MOVE IT INTO THE WALLS.
MINKA, THE MICE ARE VERY TIRED, AND SOME ARE INJURED. IS THERE A PLACE FOR THEM TO REST?
OF COURSE. THERE ARE PLENTY OF HOLES THEY CAN SLEEP IN. MAKE YOURSELVES AT HOME.
THANK YOU.
WIX? NOW WHERE ARE YOU GOING?

I HAVE TO HELP HIM.

WIX, IT'S NOT SAFE OUT HERE.
WE'LL NEVER BE SAFE WITH THOSE WOLVES OUT THERE.

YES, THAT IS TRUE.

WE CAN'T STOP EVERY PREDATOR, WIX.
BUT ATLAS CAN. RIGHT, POSSUM?

POSSIBLY.
BUT NOT WITHOUT HELP.

THEN I'M GOING TO FIND HIM.
WIX! WAIT!
UMF, MAKE SURE THE OTHERS ARE OK.
UH... YOU'RE IN CHARGE.
ME? WHERE ARE YOU GOING?
TO DRAG WIX BACK OVER HERE.

WIX! HOLD ON!
WHERE ARE YOU GOING?
I HAVE TO FIND ATLAS.
BUT YOU DON'T EVEN KNOW WHERE HE WENT.
I KNOW WHERE HE'S GOING, BUT I HAVE TO HURRY.
WHAT ARE YOU GONNA DO WHEN-
WHAT THE-!? LOOK!
BERRIES!

OMM
NOM
THESE ARE-
NOM
NOM
DELICIOUS!
OMM
NOM
NOM
THERE ARE SO MANY...
LOOK! THE SUN IS COMING OUT AGAIN.
IT DOES FEEL A BIT WARMER LATELY.
THE BERRIES... THE SUN...
DO YOU KNOW WHAT THIS MEANS!?
THE FOREST IS COMING BACK! THE WOLVES' POWER IS *WEAKENING!* NOW IS OUR CHANCE TO STOP THEM...
WIX, IT'S JUST A STORY... THEY'RE JUST ANIMALS.
NO! THIS IS A SIGN! WE HAVE TO GO! THERE ISN'T MUCH TIME.
WAIT!

HELLO, LITTLE KNIGHT.
YOU ARE LATE.
WIX?
IT'S ALRIGHT.
I THINK.
OH, HELLO.
I DIDN'T FORESEE ANOTHER MOUSE.
HI.
WITCH! I HAVE TO GET TO THE CAVE!
THAT'S PRETTY FAR AWAY.
I DON'T THINK YOU'LL MAKE IT IN TIME.
CAN YOU... CAN YOU TAKE ME THERE?
US!
ME?
TAKE YOU?
I'M NOT A MOUNT FOR RODENTS.
PLEASE? IT'S TOO FAR FOR US TO WALK.
sigh
I GUESS... JUST THIS ONCE.
TELL NO ONE ABOUT THIS.
IF ANYONE SEES US I WILL SIMPLY DIE.

MEANWHILE...
THEY JUST LEFT?
YEAH. I DON'T KNOW WHERE.
THEY GO TO THE CAVE.
THAT'S WHERE ATLAS WILL BE, IF HE CAN MAKE IT.
WE HAVE TO FIND THEM.
I DON'T KNOW...
WELL I'M GOING. CAN SOMEONE SHOW ME THE WAY?
I KNOW THE WAY.
ALRIGHT, ANYONE ELSE WHO WANTS TO GO CAN FOLLOW US.
THE REST OF YOU NEED TO GET THIS PLACE CLEANED UP AND ORGANIZED.
HOW FAR IS IT?
VERY FAR.
YOU'LL NEED HELP...
"...BUT I BELIEVE I KNOW SOME WHO CAN PROVIDE IT."

THERE!
THE CAVE!

OH NO...

THERE YOU ARE, SISTER.
ATLAS!

ARE YOU OK?

OH... IT'S YOU! I KNEW YOU'D SURVIVE.
TOLD YOU... TOLD YOU MICE WERE...TOUGHER THAN THEY... THEY LOOK.

LET'S JUST GET YOU IN THE CAVE.
I...I TRIED TO LOSE THEM IN THE RIVER...BUT IT'S NO GOOD...THEY...WILL BE HERE SOON. YOU SHOULD GO.
WHAT? NO! I'M NOT LEAVING YOU. GET UP! YOU ARE THE ONLY ONE THAT CAN STOP THEM.
ARRROOOOOOOOO
THEY'RE COMING.
THIS IS AS FAR AS I GO... YOU HAVE TO LEAVE...ME NOW.
NO!
WIX...THERE IS NOTHING WE CAN DO...
WHAT'S IN THE CAVE? THE GUARDIAN?
NO ONE MAY ENTER THE CAVE.
ONLY WHEN EREBUS IS DEAD WILL THE GUARDIAN WAKE.

WHO SAYS!?
THE VINES...THE WINDS...THE TREES...
AT LEAST... WE THINK THAT'S WHAT THEY SAY.
YOU THINK?!
WELL, THEY'RE NOT ALWAYS CLEAR...
SOMETIMES WE HAVE TO... INTERPRET.
OH, THIS IS RIDICULOUS! I'VE HEARD ENOUGH ABOUT VINES AND SKY WOLVES AND FORBIDDEN HOLES IN THE GROUND!
LOOK!
OOOOOOOOO
THEY'RE HERE.
TIME'S UP.
GOOD LUCK!
WHAT? YOU'RE LEAVING!?
COME BACK!

HMM...
I'LL NEED SOMETHING BIGGER THAN A NAIL...

WIX! COME ON! WE HAVE TO GO!
I HAVE AN IDEA...

THIS LOOKS BIG ENOUGH...

THIS IS CRAZY! I-

OH, SCREW THE RULES!

WHERE ARE YOU GOING?
TO FIND HELP!

WHAT ARE THOSE THINGS?
NO TIME TO WORRY ABOUT THAT...
GOTTA HURRY!

WIX...
IT'S TIME TO GO.
NO!
WE CAN STOP HIM.
NOT TODAY, LITTLE MOUSE.
GO TO YOUR FRIEND IN THE CAVE.
YOU'LL BE SAFE THERE.
PLEASE GET UP.
GOOOOOO...

GOODBYE, ATLAS.

HUH?

HELLO AGAIN.

YOU FOUND THE MOOSE FOR US.

ATLAS!

THE CAVE...
IT'S GETTING DARK...

AGH!

oooph!

OUCH.

gasp!

OH MY...

THE GUARDIAN...

UH... HELLO?
WE COULD USE A LITTLE HELP HERE! WAKE UP!

SHE SLEEPS...

SHE WILL ONLY AWAKE WHEN THE--

--WHEN THE SHADOW IS DEAD. YEAH, YEAH, I GOT ALL THAT!

HAS EVERYONE LOST THEIR MINDS?!

MEANWHILE...
MOOSE FLESH!
BACK!
I EAT FIRST.
STAY BACK!
YOU ARE GOING TO STOP ME?
OK THEN.
STOP ME.

EEP!
GAAAAKH!

KOFF!
KOFF!
KOFF!
GASP!
GRRRR...
I WAS GOING TO SWALLOW YOU WHOLE...
...NOW I'LL TEAR YOU TO PIECES!
I'LL CRUSH YOUR BONES!
I'LL...
YOU'LL REGRET COMING HERE!
?
RAAARRRGH!

THE CAVE...
OH NO... WIX!

WAKE UP!
WAKE UP!
WAKE UP!

GOOO... AWAYYY...

OUTSIDE.
GGGRRRRRAHH!

OOOH!

HUFF
HUFF
HUFF

HUFF
KOFF!
KOFF!

KOFF!
KOFF!
KOFF!
KOFF!
KOFF!

EREBUS IS INJURED...
WEAKNESSSSS...

WHAT?

I'M... KOFF! KOFF! I'M FINE!

BACK!
STAY BACK!

AGH!

RUSTLE
RUSTLE
RUSTLE
YELP
SNAP!
SNARL
TEAR
RIP!
GRRRR
WIX...
SORRY ABOUT THIS...
POKE!

EEK!
I SAID GO AWAY!

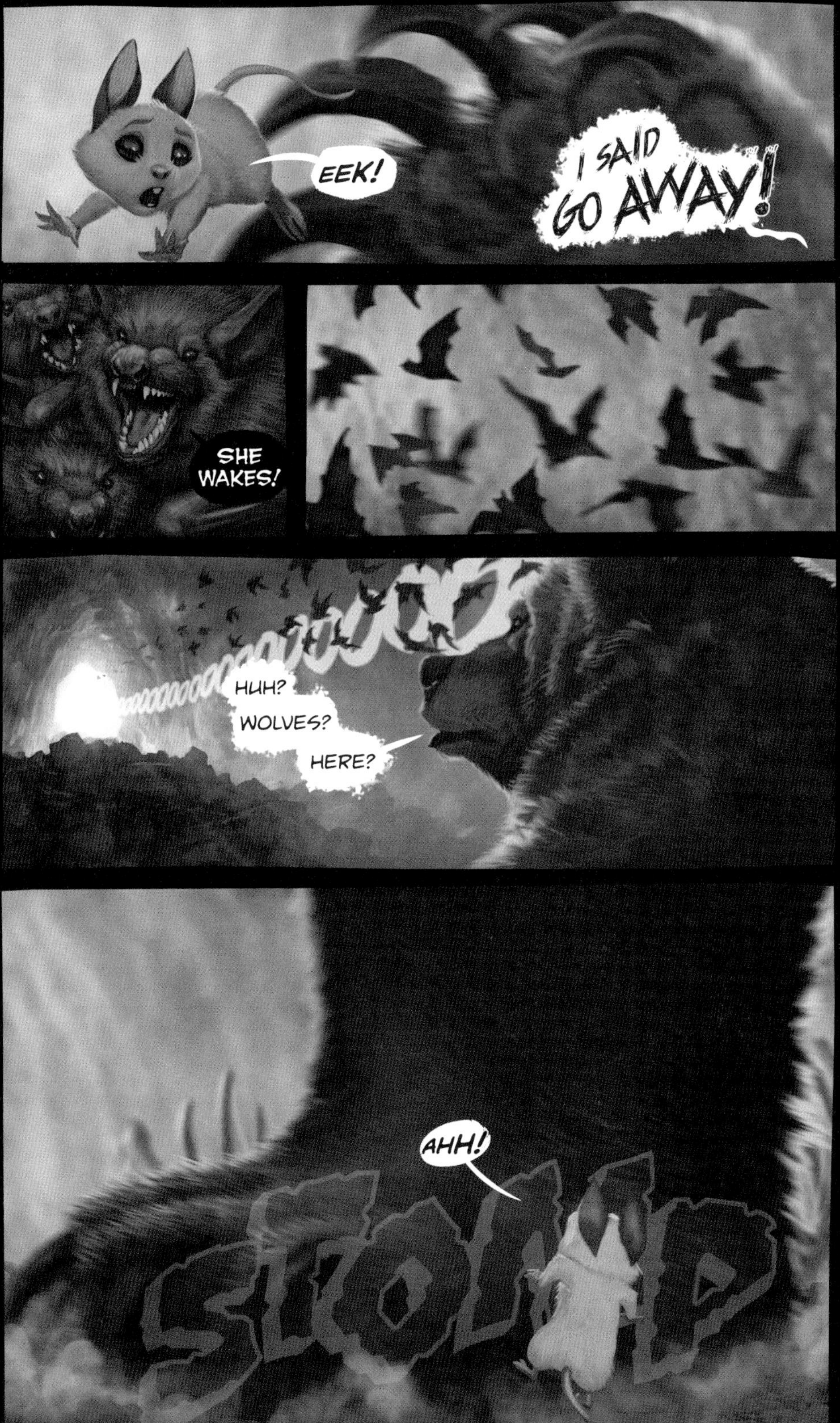

SHE WAKES!

HUH?
WOLVES?
HERE?

AHH!
STOMP

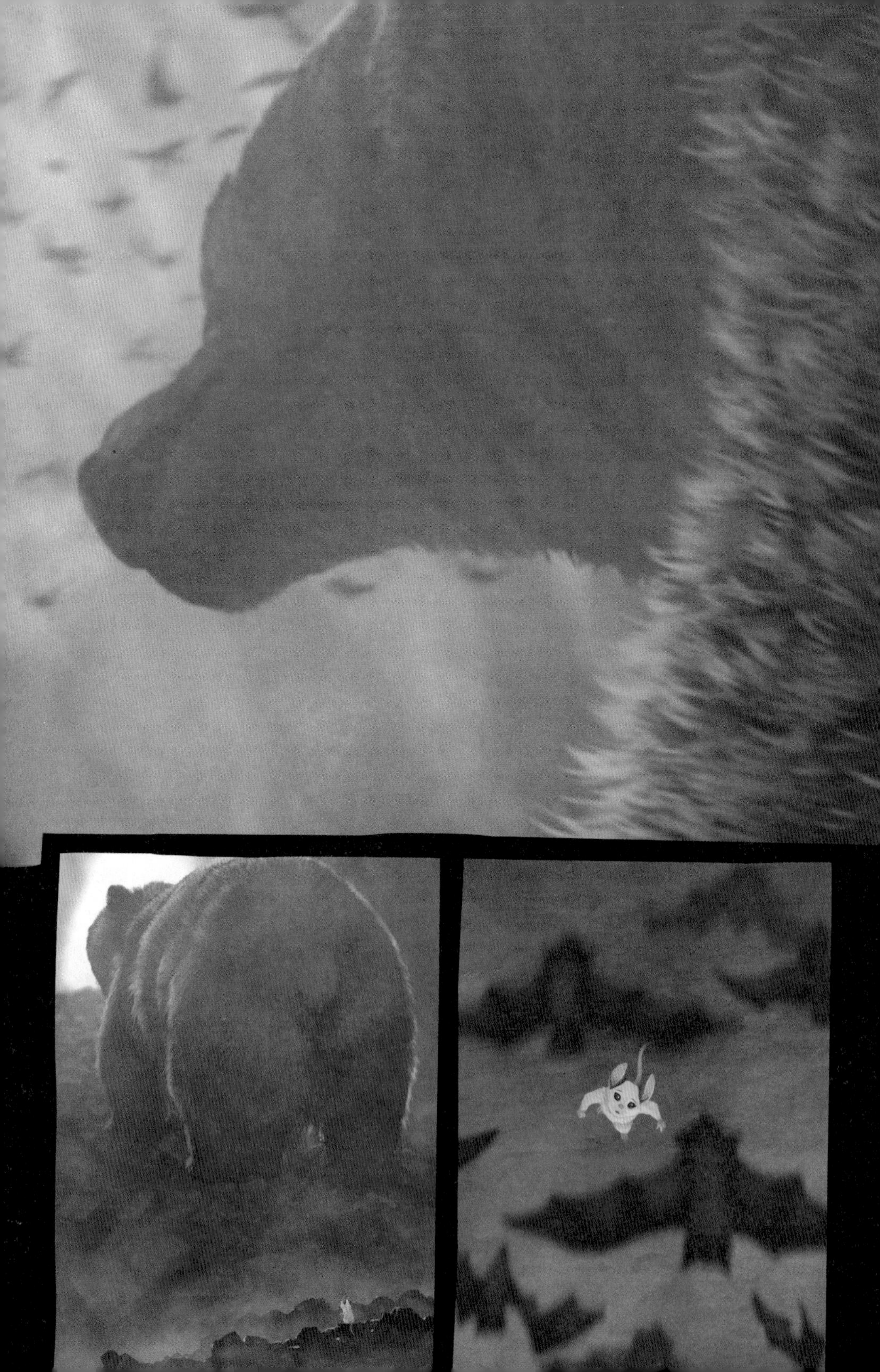

WAIT FOR ME!

ERBUS IS DEAD!
GOOD!

NOW I WILL LEAD!
NO! IT SHOULD BE ME!
NO! ME!

SILENCE!

YOU ARE ALL TOO WEAK!

I AM KING NOW!

THERE ARE NO KINGS HERE.

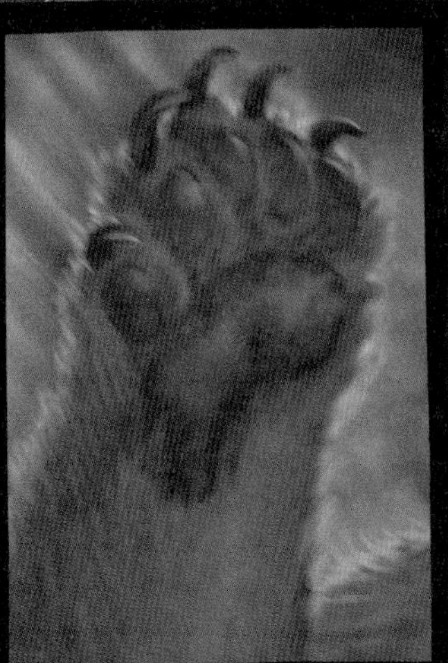

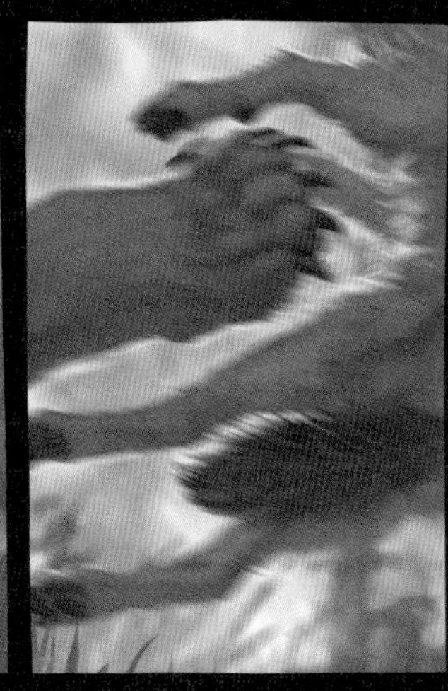

CRACK!

BLEH...!

ROOOAR!!!

YELP!

RUN!

RAAHRRR!!!

WIX?
OH NO.
THERE THEY ARE!

WE'RE TOO LATE.

WIX...

...

ARE THEY GONE YET?

FAKER!
OOF!
HEY!

THEY'RE OK!

ATLAS?
-MMM-
THEY'RE GONE.
...OH?
...GOOD...
I THINK I'LL REST ...HERE AWHILE...
LOOK!
IT'S COMING BACK!
THE WITCHES!
WHAT ARE THEY TALKING ABOUT?
I DON'T KNOW...
BUT SHE'S COMING OVER HERE!

REST EASY, ATLAS. I WILL NOT HARM YOU.
THOSE STRANGE FOXES SAY SOMETHING ABOUT A CURSE...

I'M TOLD I HAVE THIS MOUSE TO THANK FOR BREAKING IT AND WAKING ME...

...THOUGH I THINK HE MIGHT HAVE HAD SOME HELP WITH THAT.

I UH... SORRY ABOUT THE NOSE.
HUH?

THE WITCHES THINK I CAN CONTROL THE WEATHER...
...THAT I CAN MAKE IT WARMER AND STOP THE POISONED WINDS.
IF I COULD DO THAT, MY LITTLE PRINCE WOULD STILL BE WITH ME...

"BUT I THINK THE WEATHER CHANGES ANYWAY. THE RIVER FLOWS AGAIN. FISH WILL COME SOON...
"...AND I AM HUNGRY."

THE WOLVES WILL NOT RETURN...
...YOU WILL BE SAFE HERE IN MY FOREST...FOR A TIME...
...AS SAFE AS YOUR KIND CAN BE.
GOODBYE.

SOMETIME LATER...
LOOK AT THAT, SIS.
THEY ARE THRIVING SO QUICKLY!
"LOOK HOW ORGANIZED THEY ARE!
"SOME ARE MOVING OUT TO START NEW NESTS.
"AND LOOK AT HOW CLEVER THEY ARE GETTING!
"THEY ARE LEARNING NEW TRICKS!"
HOW DID THEY FIGURE OUT HOW TO OPEN THOSE CANS?
HOW DID WE LEARN TO READ THE TREES?
WE ARE CHANGING.
WHO CARES?!
THEY LOOK SO...
TASTY!

NOW, SISTER, THE HUNT HAS TO WAIT.
WE PROMISED THE GUARDIAN THAT WE WOULD GIVE THEM TIME TO BUILD UP THEIR NUMBERS.
YES, YES. WE WILL WAIT...
BUT I WISH THAT POACHER WOULD GO AWAY!
THE INTERLOPER!
GET OUT OF HERE, STUPID HAWK!
THIS IS OUR LAND NOW!
ENOUGH, SISTER. WE HAVE OTHER PLACES TO BE!
YES! OTHER THINGS TO DO!
GOODBYE FOR NOW, LITTLE MICE!
ARE YOU SURE YOU WON'T STAY?
NAH! WE ARE FOREST MICE. IT'S TOO STUFFY IN THERE.
BESIDES, THE WOODS HAVE DRIED OUT AND THE PLANTS ARE GROWING BACK. WE'LL BE FINE.
WANT TO JOIN US?
ONE DAY SOON, PERHAPS. FOR NOW I HAVE TO HELP THE COLONY GET BACK ON ITS FEET.
STILL LOTS OF WORK TO DO.
BE WELL, HOUSE MOUSE.
LET US KNOW IF YOU NEED ANYTHING.
PICT!

THE LAST OF TODAY'S FORAGING IS BEING TUCKED AWAY NOW.
LOOKS LIKE WE'LL HAVE ENOUGH TO LAST A WHILE.
GREAT! THANK YOU.
WAIT!

NOT ALL OF IT.

HEY, PICT!

WE FOUND ALL KINDS OF STUFF IN A DUMPSTER A FEW BLOCKS AWAY. MOST OF IT IS EDIBLE I THINK.
WE ALSO FOUND SOME MORE BERRIES ON THE WAY BACK!

THERE'S TONS OF THEM OUT THERE!
ABOUT TIME YOU SHOWED UP!
WE FIGURED YOU WERE EATEN BY NOW.
ATLAS, YOU WERE SUPPOSED TO KEEP HIM ON SCHEDULE!

SORRY ABOUT THAT, MISS PICT.
HEY, WIX, CAN YOU GET THIS STUFF OFF ME?
I'M STARTING TO SMELL LIKE GARBAGE.
OH, YEAH! NO PROBLEM.
COME ON, UMF, LET'S UNLOAD THE LOOT.
LOOK OUT BELOW!
ALRIGHT, MICE. LET'S GET THIS SORTED AND PUT AWAY.
THANKS FOR ALL YOUR HELP, ATLAS.
HOW ARE YOU FEELING?
OH, I'M OK. STILL A LITTLE SORE, BUT I'LL BE FINE.

I'M STARVING! COME ON, WIX, LET'S GET SOME GRUB!
I'LL JOIN YOU LATER, UMF. ME AND ATLAS STILL HAVE TO PATROL THE FOREST.
COME ON, PICT! LET'S GO FOR A RIDE.
OH, I STILL HAVE A LOT OF WORK TO DO AROUND HERE.
WE STILL HAVE TO GET THIS STUFF PUT AWAY BEFORE DARK.

WE CAN HANDLE IT, MISS.
YOU GO AHEAD.
OH... UH...OK THEN.
WATCH YOUR STEP!

READY?
READY.
OK, LET'S GO, ATLAS!
OK, OFF WE GO!

TO BE
CONTINUED...

CHARACTERS OF SCURRY

THE COLONY

WIX — MOUSE

Despite his small stature, Wix is one of the best scavengers in the Colony. He is deceptively fast and can avoid traps and poison better than any other mouse...but his overconfidence and impatience can get him into trouble.

PICT — MOUSE

Pict is a spirited and intelligent mouse, raised by her father Orim to lead the Colony when he is gone. While she cares dutifully for her father, she often wishes she could explore the outside world like her friend Wix.

UMF — RAT

Generally, rats and mice do not get along, but Umf won over the Colony of mice with his friendly and unassuming disposition. He became close friends with Wix after a particularly dangerous scavenging run, and the two have been partners ever since.

ORIM — MOUSE

Master Orim is the wise and fair leader of the Colony. Ancient by mouse standards, Orim has led the mice through many difficult years, but many are whispering that he has become too cautious.

KESSEL — MOUSE

Kessel is Orim's right hand and captain of the scouts and guards. He has worked tirelessly to safeguard the Colony since it was created, and leads the most important scouting missions personally.

RESHER — MOUSE

Resher is the head of a western nest of mice who reluctantly joined the Colony after a fire destroyed their home. He is an extremely large, ambitious and power-hungry mouse, adept at gaining followers and resources.

AKAMA — RAT

Akama is not a member of the mouse Colony, she is an emissary of the Shade Run rats, a mysterious and reclusive group of rats who control the northern end of the Neighborhood. She is very curious about mouse society.

UTT — MOUSE

Utt is the vain and corrupt overseer of the storerooms. He isn't terribly bright, but wants what's best for the Colony, if only for his own survival.

MOTTLE — MOUSE

Mottle is a young orphan mouse who spends most of her time rummaging through the storeroom looking for tasty bits to eat. She dreams of becoming a scavenger or scout one day like her hero, Wix.

SKEK — MOUSE

Skek is Resher's number one henchman. Cantankerous and foul smelling even by mouse standards, he spends his time away from the others, usually skulking in the Colony house's basement.

THE ELDER COUNCIL

The Elder Council is made up of the original leaders of the first five nests that formed the Colony, with Master Orim as its head. They do not wield absolute power but are greatly respected and hold much influence over the Colony.

THE CATS

TITAN — CAT

Titan is a large, powerful cat with razor sharp claws and a fiery tortoiseshell coat (a rarity for a male). Born a sickly stray, he grew up to be a massive beast and a great hunter. Now the unquestioned leader of the cats, he rules with brutality. Only one mouse has ever escaped his clutches... and Titan has never forgotten.

ORK — CAT

Ork was a spoiled and well-groomed Himalayan house cat before being abandoned by her owners. They didn't even remove her collar and bell before they left. This has made it difficult for her to survive on her own, as her bell warns any mice away long before she can sneak up on them.

SCRATCHER — CAT

Scratcher is a young stray who has grown up without relying on humans for food. He has speed and agility to make up for his small size, and though he's not particularly bright, he has enough craftiness to occasionally sneak up on something.

Gizz and Fig are usually too lazy to go hunting with the others. They prefer lounging around during the day, and rummaging for scraps when they get hungry, though they'll happily chase any mouse that comes their way.

THE OTHERS

NEMESIS HARRIS'S HAWK

Nemesis the Harris's hawk silently glides through the mists in search of prey for her chicks, and the Neighborhood has become her favorite hunting ground.

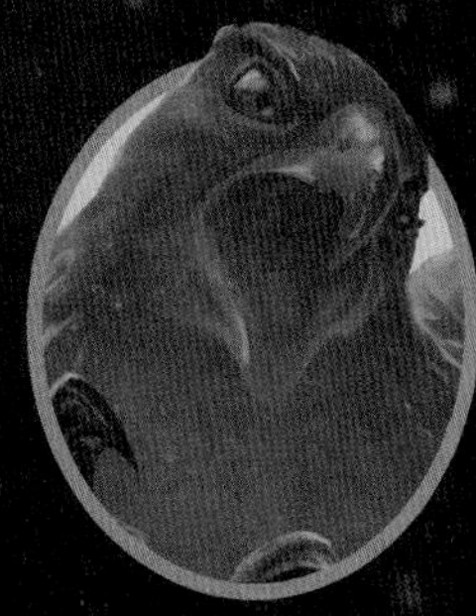

EREBUS WOLF

A mysterious wolf who prowls the woods near the Neighborhood houses. Erebus and his pack haven't dared to enter the neighborhood for fear of the humans, but now that the humans are gone...

THE WOLVES

Led by Erebus, a great wolf pack has invaded from the woods to the east. They stayed away because of a powerful guardian that protected the woods, but in its absence, they laid claim to the entire land as their hunting ground.

SNAG DOUGLAS SQUIRREL

Snag is a cantankerous old Douglas Squirrel who lived deep in the woods until they became flooded. Now a resident of the Refuge, he lives in trunk of a dead tree on the southern edge of the island.

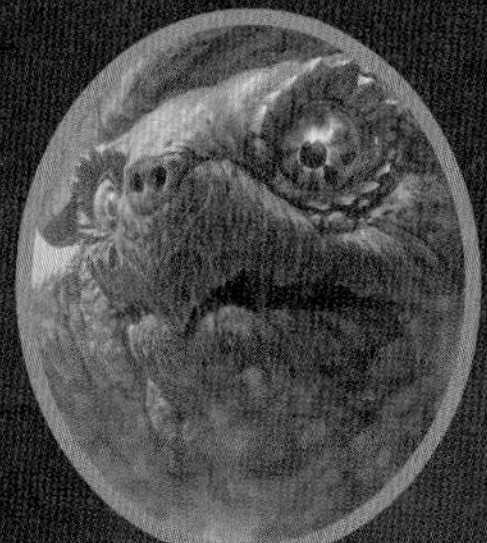

SKOGA SNAPPER TURTLE

Skoga is a large and ancient snapper turtle who has lived in the woods longer than any other living creature. He hates to be disturbed.

ARKEN BEAVER

Arken is the Master Engineer and Architect of the Beaver dam. His knowledge of dam building is unmatched among the beavers, but even he is hard pressed to meet his king's unreasonable demands.

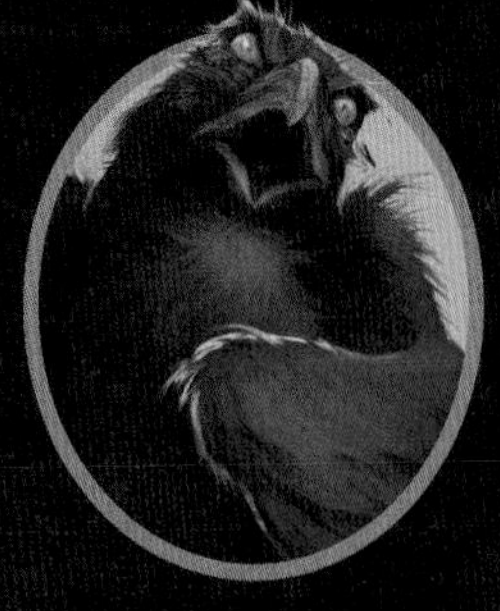

NYLL RAVEN

Nyll is the leader of the mysterious ravens and head advisor to the king of the beavers. In return for food from the refugees' stores, the ravens act as the beavers' eyes and ears in the forest and oversee the workers at the dam.

ATLAS MOOSE

Atlas is a great moose from the east. Most of the surviving moose, deer and elk moved away to avoid the wolves, but Atlas went west towards the city, in search of a mysterious guardian who may be the key to saving the forest.

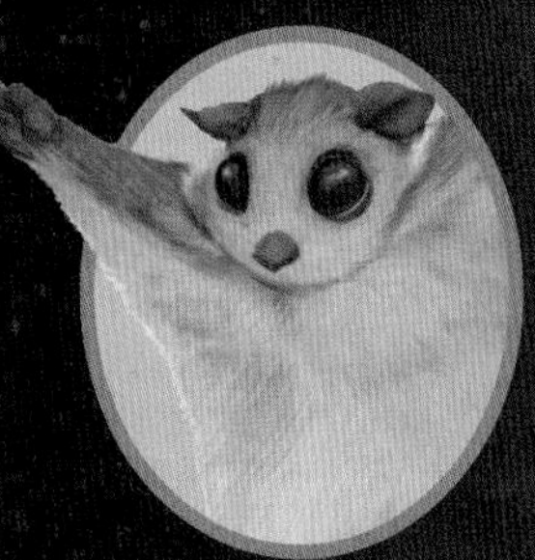

FLIK FLYING SQUIRREL

Flik is a flying squirrel who hangs out with the forest mice, who she finds more friendly than the solitary tree squirrels. She has little to fear from wolves or other land predators but takes pity on her earthbound friends.

GORGON NORTHERN WATER SNAKE

Gorgon is a Northern Water Snake who makes her home in a plastic kiddie pool discarded by the humans. The cold water makes her sluggish, but she is still more than capable of hunting anything that crosses her path.

KING SHONK — BEAVER

King Shonk is king of the beavers. Once a wise and able leader, in recent years he has become ambitious and foul tempered, obsessed with his mad quest to build the largest dam ever.

THE REFUGEES

The refugees are a ragtag group of forest animals who were moved to a swampy island by the beavers after their forest was flooded.

THE WITCHES — FOXES

The witches are a strange trio of fox sisters who silently stalk the forest, making their presence known only when they choose and manipulating events for their own purpose.

THE POSSUM

The Possum has seen and heard much in his wanderings through the cities, suburbs and forests, but the strange stories he tells can be hard to believe.

BONUS PREQUEL

ABANDONED

"YOU SURE THIS IS THE HOUSE THAT WE'RE SUPPOSED TO SCAVENGE, WIX?"
"YEAH, THIS IS THE PLACE."
"IT LOOKS LIKE IT'S ABOUT TO COLLAPSE."
THEY ALWAYS GIVE US THE WORST ONES. SOME OF THE NEARBY HOUSES LOOK MORE PROMISING.
WE HAVE TO STICK TO THE HOUSES WE WERE ASSIGNED.
BUT ONE OF THE OTHER HOUSES MIGHT STILL HAVE HUMANS INSIDE. AND WHERE THERE'S HUMANS, THERE'S FOOD.
NO HUMANS LEFT AROUND HERE, UMF.
STRANGE...
...NO ANIMALS AROUND HERE EITHER ... NOT EVEN A CAT.
LET'S GET INSIDE. WE CAN GET IN THROUGH THE BROKEN WINDOW UP THERE.

CAREFUL WITH THE GLASS, UMF.
SEE ANYTHING?
LOOKS LIKE THE PLACE HAS BEEN LOOTED ALREADY...
...BUT MAYBE WE CAN FIND SOMETHING THEY MISSED.

I HOPE SO...I'M STARVING!
LET'S TRY THE PANTRY.
EMPTY.
ugh!
I'M SO HUNGRY.
GRRRRRR...
YEAH, I KNOW. I CAN HEAR YOUR STOMACH GROWL--
gasp!
DOG!

RUN!

RUN WHERE!?
BARK!
BARK!
BARK!
BARK!
BARK!
BARK!

HUH?
BARK!
BARK!
BARK!
BARK!

WOAH!
EASY, GIRL!
EASY...

QUIET DOWN, DOLLY! THEY'LL HEAR YOU!
shh... EASY...

WHO ARE YOU?
I'M CALLED MOBLEY. IF YOU'VE COME LOOKING FOR FOOD, I'M AFRAID YOU WON'T FIND ANY HERE

WE'VE EATEN ALL THAT WAS LEFT BEHIND AFTER THE HUMAN WENT AWAY.
WE THOUGHT THIS PLACE WAS ABANDONED.
I WISH IT WAS. WE'VE BEEN TRAPPED IN HERE FOR AGES.
I COULD SLIP OUT EASY ENOUGH, BUT I CAN'T LEAVE WITHOUT MY FRIEND DOLLY HERE...
IF NOT FOR HER, I'D STILL BE STUCK IN THAT CAGE.
THERE'S GOTTA BE ANOTHER WAY OUT OF HERE...
HUH?
BUMP!
SNIFF SNIFF SNIFF
THUMP!
SOMETHING'S OUTSIDE!

BANG!
SCRATCH
SCRATCH
SCRATCH
THEY'RE BACK!
WHO'S BACK?
BANG!
BAD DOGS. A WHOLE PACK OF THEM.
BANG!
THEY'VE BEEN SNIFFING AROUND OUTSIDE FOR DAYS, TRYING TO GET IN.
IT'S LIKE THEY'VE BEEN DRIVEN MAD.
BUMP!
BUMP!
BUMP!
BANG!
BANG!
GRRRRR...
SCRATCH
SCRATCH
SCRATCH
BANG!
BAM!
CRACK!

THAT DOOR IS OLD AND CRACKED.
IT WON'T HOLD MUCH LONGER!
WE HAVE TO HIDE!
COME ON, DOLLY! TIME TO GO!
IT'LL TAKE FOREVER TO GET BACK UP THERE...
NO TIME! FOLLOW US TO THE BACK ROOM. WE DON'T USUALLY GO IN THERE, BUT IT LOOKS LIKE WE HAVE NO CHOICE...
BOOM!
OK...
WAIT! WHY DON'T YOU GO BACK THERE?

BANG! BANG! BANG!
CRACK!
PING!
WAM!
SNIFF SNIFF SNIFF
SNIFF SNIFF
GRRRRR..
NO, DOLLY! TURN AROUND!

YELP!
GO! GO! GO!
COME ON, WIX!
HEY!

HANG ON!

BARK!
BARK!
BARK!
yelp!
yelp!
yelp!

BARK!
BARK!
BARK!
BARK!
QUICKLY!

HURRY! SHUT THE DOOR!
hrrgh!

CLICK!
pant!
pant!
pant!
phew!

BUMP!
SCRATCH
SCRATCH
I HOPE THIS DOOR HOLDS BETTER THAN THE OTHER ONE.
DON'T COUNT ON IT. LET'S FIND A WAY OUT OF HERE.
SCRATCH
SCRATCH
SCRATCH
CREEPY CAGES UP THERE. WHAT IS THIS PLACE?
THE BIRD ROOM.
A HAUNTED PLACE.
OUR HUMAN COLLECTED MANY BIRDS FROM ALL OVER THE WORLD.
THEY USED TO CHIRP ALL DAY...
...BUT NOW THE CAGES ARE SILENT.
scratch
scritch
scratch
HEY... WHAT'S SHE SCRATCHING AT OVER THERE?
hMMM... IT'S TOO BAD YOU NEVER CAME IN HERE...
I THINK YOUR FRIEND HAS FOUND A WAY OUT!
THERE'S A BOARDED UP DOG DOOR BACK HERE!
IT'S OLD AND ROTTEN LIKE EVERYTHING ELSE...
HELP ME PRY IT OFF!
CREEEAK

hrrrghfff!
WATCH THE NAILS!
COME ON, GIRL! YOU CAN MAKE IT!
LOOKS LIKE WE'RE IN THE CLEAR.
WE'RE OUT, DOLLY! WE'RE FINALLY FREE!
WE BETTER GET OUTTA HERE BEFORE THE DOGS NOTICE WE'RE NOT INSIDE.
HEY, MOBLEY, YOU WANT TO GO WITH US BACK TO THE COLONY? I'M SURE WE CAN FIND A PLACE FOR YOU AND YOUR FRIEND. A GUARD DOG MIGHT COME IN HANDY...
oof ...THANKS, BUT ME AND DOLLY HAVE BEEN STUCK INSIDE LONG ENOUGH.
I THINK WE'LL HEAD SOUTH AND SEE WHAT WE CAN DIG UP.
I SEE... WELL, GOOD LUCK TO YOU TWO!
AND HURRY! YOU'LL NEED TO PUT SOME SPACE BETWEEN YOU AND THOSE DOGS.
WILL DO. SO LONG, FRIENDS!

WELL, I GUESS WE SHOULD GET BACK HOME...
...THEY'LL BE WONDERING WHERE WE ARE.
=sigh= EMPTY HANDED AGAIN...
NO...
YA KNOW...THERE ARE PLENTY OF OTHER HOUSES AROUND HERE. THERE'S GOTTA BE *SOMETHING* IN ONE OF THEM.
BUT WE WEREN'T ASSIGNED...
WHO CARES? ONCE WE FIND SOME GOOD LOOT, IT WON'T MATTER WHERE WE FOUND IT!
COME ON! LET'S CHECK 'EM OUT.
END.

MAC SMITH is a self-taught comic artist living in the Pacific Northwest with his extremely furry dog. He also creates concept art for studios such as Blizzard, Warner Bros., Games Workshop, and Bethesda. SCURRY is his debut graphic novel. More of his work can be found at mac-smith.com.

READING GUIDE

IMPORTANT SETTINGS

- The Colony
- The Forest
- The Refuge
- Beaver Dam
- The Cave

KEY THEMES

- Survival
- Betrayal & Friendship
- Community
- Power & Corruption
- Change vs Tradition
- Courage & Heroism

IMPORTANT CHARACTERS

- Wix - Mouse
- Umf - Rat
- Pict - Mouse
- Master Orim- Mouse
- Kessel - Mouse
- Resher - Mouse
- Titan - Cat
- Mottle - Mouse
- Skek - Mouse
- Snag - Squirrel
- Skoga - Snapper Turtle
- Arken - Beaver
- Atlas - Moose
- King Shonk - Beaver
- Nyll - Raven
- Minka - Mouse
- Erebus - Wolf
- Flik - Flying Squirrel
- Akama - Rat
- The Witches - Foxes
- Possum - Possum
- The Guardian - Fabled Protector of the Forest

DISCUSSION QUESTIONS

1. When Possum speaks of the war that ended human habitation of the environment, he refers to a "Fire Wolf" and "Sky Wolf" that wrought mass destruction. To what is he actually referring? Why does he use the "wolf" metaphor?
2. The Colony must decide whether to continue with traditions or make a radical change that will be the best for their future. Think of a time when you faced making a decision involving a major change and the outcome was uncertain. How did you make that decision?
3. Provide two examples where a character's facial expression enhanced your understanding of what they were saying. Give two examples when the expressions helped you understand the emotions of a panel/the story where there were no words.
4. Give two examples of how individual strength and courage helped characters survive in this world. Give two examples of how working together and collective action aided their survival.
5. What do you think Wix's dreams represent? How do they affect his journey?
6. How did the dreams foreshadow future events in the book?
7. The book utilizes flashbacks to recount information about this fantasy world and the legend of The Guardian. How did the art in these sections differ from depictions of scenes happening in the present? Which panel from a dream/flashback was your favorite, and why?

DISCUSSION QUESTIONS

8. Towards the story's end, The Witches note The Colony member's ability to open cans and read trees and say "We are changing". What do you think they meant by this? How does this fit into the book's setting?

9. Despite the characters speaking and acting in sometimes human ways, they also behave like their animal species. Give three examples where a character personified their species in words or actions.

10. Describe two different action sequences in the book and how the art enhanced those sections. Pick your two favorite panels from these action sequences and explain why you liked them.

11. Near the end of the story Wix and Pict have differing opinions about the prophecies and signs surrounding the fate of the forest. How do their differing views contribute to their actions in the final confrontation?

12. Despite having limited experience away from The Colony, Pict displays a great deal of courage. Pick an example of dialogue that highlights Pict's bravery despite the danger of her travels.

ACTIVITY IDEAS

1. The animals in SCURRY have varying opinions on how they will survive. Imagine you were a mouse or rat with the group. Write a short story of what you'd do to persuade the group to stay, to go, or introduce and describe a third option.
2. Art is a major component in telling the story of SCURRY. Pick a time before the story took place, events that might have happened during the story, a prophecy the Witches have yet to tell, or anything else. Paint, draw, or create an art piece that tells more of the story that hasn't been seen yet or would help the story make more sense.
3. Identify what you think is the biggest theme of the book (use themes from this guide or come up with your own). Pick five panels in SCURRY that best represent your chosen theme. You can choose panels for either art or dialogue. Prepare a brief explanation how each panel represents the theme, and prepare to share it in class.
4. You have been hired to create a soundtrack for SCURRY. Choose songs to feature in the soundtrack; either write them down or create an actual playlist. Think of at least three specific parts of the book and which song you would want to play as people read those parts. Briefly explain why you chose each song. For example, what song would pair well with the story's finale?

Special thanks to my agent, Gordon Warnock, editor Alex Antone, and the legendary Don Bluth.

Mac Smith: *Creator, Writer, Artist, Letterer*
Alex Antone: *Collection Editor*
Jillian Crab: *Collection Design + Production*

Teaching guide by **Creators, Assemble Inc.** | Lexile Measure: GN240L

SCURRY. FIRST PRINTING. 978-1-5343-2436-7
Published by Image Comics, Inc. Office of Publication: PO BOX 14457, Portland, OR 97293.

SKYBOUND
COMET

image

The Domed City
of MEGA 416.

KOBUSHI
SALVAGE
KEEP

KRAK

HAAAA!!!

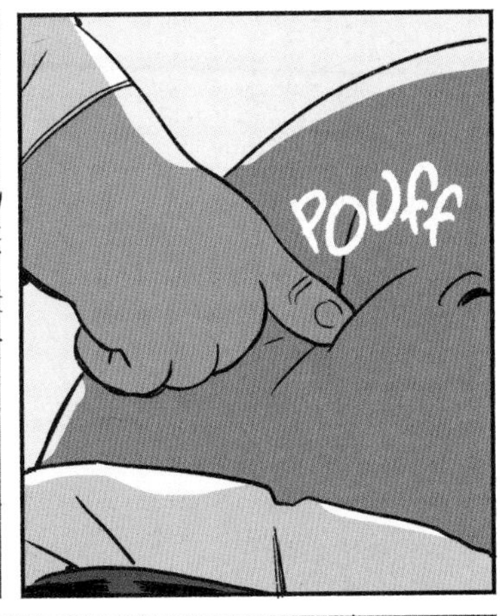
POUFF

GOH!
What is this?
DOINK
DOINK

You're almost as fat as the *stray!*
rrrmyah

Mei... the dojo's been closed for years.

We're *old!* We've earned some time to relax.

I see.
I guess relaxing is more important than...

Spaghetti?

We're all out of tomatoes.
Say no more, I'll go to Mr. Hound's!

I'll be back before you know it.
Thank you, honey.

HOUND'S
CONVENIENC

ZZZzz..SNRT! ZZZzzz

Heh, heh.
CLINK

Now, there's a man who understands relaxation.
ZZZ~

Tweet tweet TWEET

TWEEEEEEET

Tweee~~.
What in the world's got you all worked up?

SKASH

...
Oh.

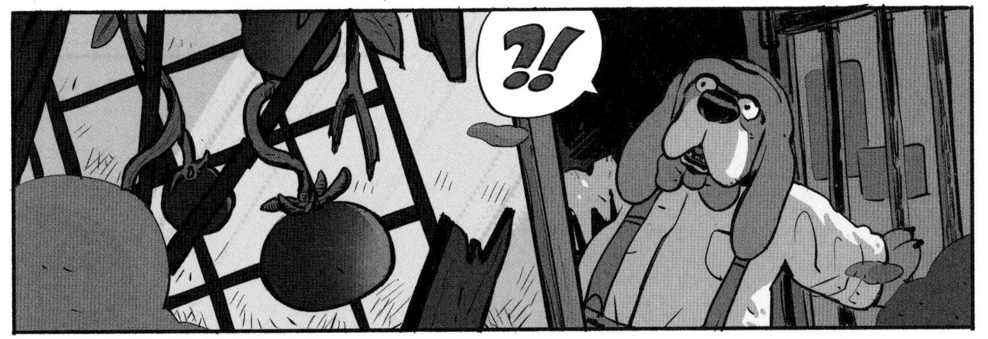

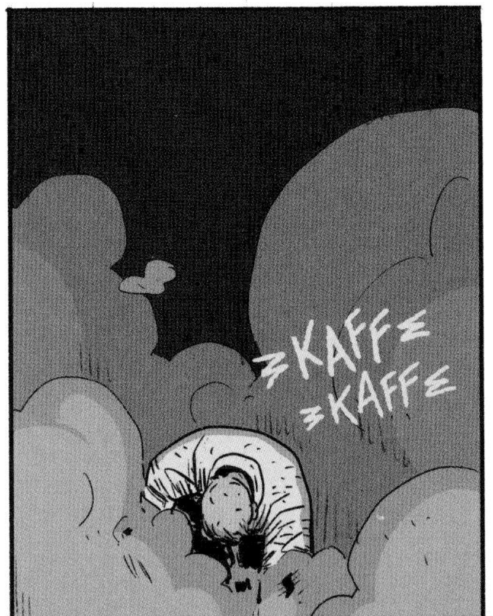

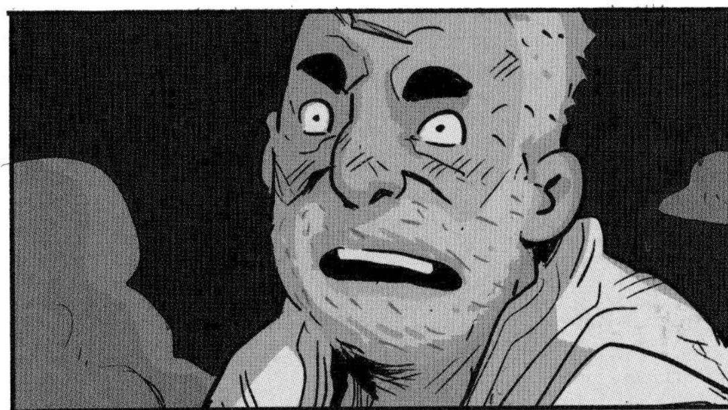

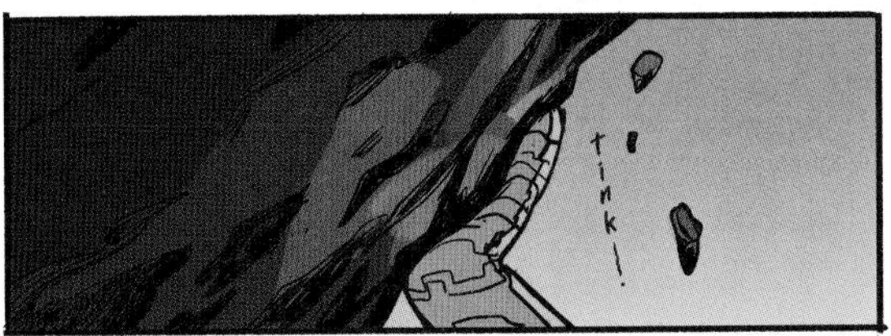

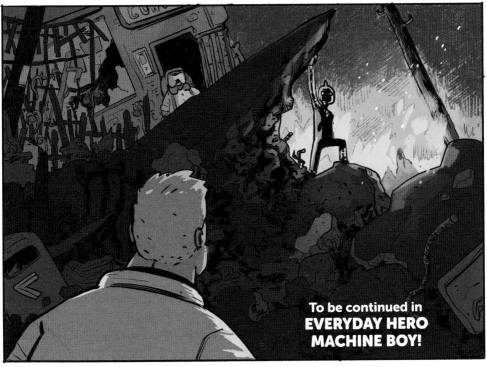

To be continued in
EVERYDAY HERO MACHINE BOY!

EXPLORE NEW WO[obscured by label]

For Middle Grade Readers in **SKYBOUND COMET**

A 10-year-old genius and his T-Rex best friend!

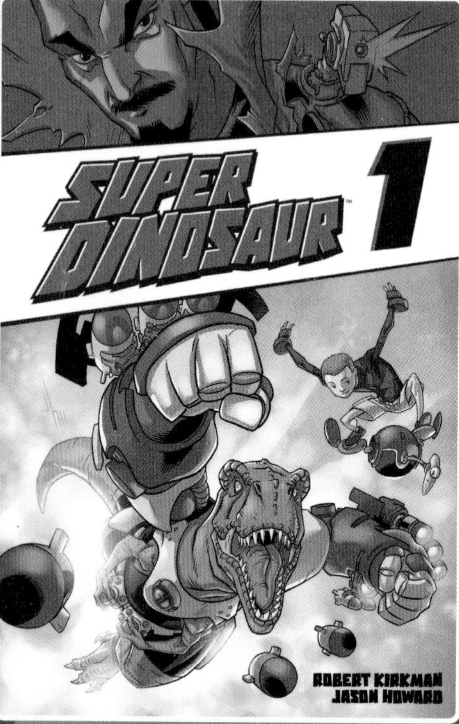

ON SALE NOW!

Vol. 1 • ISBN: 978-1-6070-6420-6 • $9.99
Vol. 2 • ISBN: 978-1-6070-6568-5 • $12.99
Vol. 3 • ISBN: 978-1-6070-6667-5 • $12.99
Vol. 4 • ISBN: 978-1-6070-6843-3 • $12.99

Activate your heart. Be an Everyday Hero!

"*Astro Boy* meets *The Iron Giant*, a sweet, funny, action-packed story for every sci-fi loving young reader!"

-FAITH ERIN HICKS
(Avatar: The Last Airbender, The Nameless City)

IRMA KNIIVILA TRI VUONG

ON SALE NOW!

ISBN: 978-1-5343-2130-4 • $12.99

Visit **SkyboundComet.com** for more information, previews, teaching guides and more!

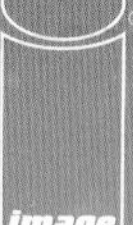